"Could you remove the sunglasses, sir?" the security checker asked.

"Of course."

Annalise had the strongest urge to turn around so she could look into his eyes, but practicality took over. What she saw there could have no bearing upon her.

As she tugged her cart it turned sideways, crashing into this man who made her feel things she didn't want to feel. If she were only as graceful as she was independent.

"Sorry." She meant for her gaze to skitter across his face, but his eyes ensnared hers.

Tiger eyes. Amber-golden with specks of brown, rimmed in a darker brown. Tiger eyes with a depth of—sorrow?—behind the brightness.

"No problem."

He blinked, releasing her and allowing her to blink as well. When he raised an eyebrow at her she realized she'd been staring.

Flustered, she yanked her cart, banging into the counter and almost taking out the passenger scanner. He must think her a total klutz.

What did it matter what he thought? Odds were they would never see each other again unless he had a medical emergency. And he certainly looked healthy to her. Well-worn jeans and a wrinkled T-shirt couldn't hide his physical fitness.

She bumped into passengers all the time. None of them elicited a significant response from her.

Annalise overcame the impulse to check him out one more time.

What was it about him that made her feel...? What? Aware? Self-conscious? Tingly? That made her feel anything at all?

Dear Reader

When cruise ship doctor Annalise Walcott first sees celebrity surgeon Niko Christopoulos she thinks he must be a swimsuit model. But, like the ocean, Niko is more than he appears to be on the surface.

Annalise has her own uneasily buried secrets that only a man used to braving the depths of human tragedy—a man like Niko—can possibly bring to the surface.

Will love be enough to give these two the strength to survive the stormy wreckage of their pasts and build a bright future under the sun together?

Wishing you calm winds and gentle seas.

Connie

P.S. I'd love to visit with you!
Find me on Facebook, www.facebook.com/
   ConnieCox.writer,
on Twitter, @conniecox,
on Goodreads, www.goodreads.com/Connie_Cox,
and on my website, www.conniecox.com

HIS HIDDEN AMERICAN BEAUTY

BY
CONNIE COX

MILLS
BOON

First published in Great Britain 2013
by Mills & Boon, an imprint of Harlequin (UK) Limited.
Large Print edition 2013
Harlequin (UK) Limited, Eton House,
18-24 Paradise Road, Richmond, Surrey TW9 1SR

© Connie Cox 2013

ISBN: 978 0 263 23132 8

Printed and bound in Great Britain
by CPI Antony Rowe, Chippenham, Wiltshire

Connie Cox has loved Harlequin Mills & Boon romances since she was a young teen. To be a Harlequin Mills & Boon author now is a fantasy come to life. By training, Connie is an electrical engineer. Through her first job, working on nuclear scanners and other medical equipment, she had a unique perspective on the medical world. She is fascinated by the inner strength of medical professionals, who must balance emotional compassion with stoic logic, and is honoured to showcase the passion of these dedicated professionals through her own passion of writing. Married to the boy-next-door, Connie is the proud mother of one terrific daughter and son-in-law and one precocious dachshund.

Connie would love to hear from you. Visit her website at www.ConnieCox.com

Recent titles by Connie Cox:

THE BABY WHO SAVED DR CYNICAL
RETURN OF THE REBEL SURGEON

**Available in eBook format
from www.millsandboon.co.uk**

CHAPTER ONE

DR. ANNALISE WALCOTT adjusted the two huge cases of medicines on her cart before she made the steep climb up the gangplank of the luxury cruise liner *Neptune's Fantasy*. While she'd had most of the supplies delivered straight to her onboard facilities, she liked to bring along the ones that needed refrigeration herself, just to make sure they stayed at the correct temperature. Not that she'd ever had a problem—Annalise avoided problems as often as she could.

Call her a control freak and she wouldn't deny it. She'd learned a long time ago that the only person she could consistently rely on was herself.

She trailed behind the last-minute stragglers, crewmates eking out the final seconds of shore leave before they boarded for the transatlantic cruise. They would be out at sea for over ten days straight before the first port of call, which meant a lot fewer breaks for the staff. And only a small percentage of crew got shore leave at each port.

With rotating days off, most of them wouldn't have a personal day on land for at least four weeks.

One by one, they went through Security, a procedure that took forever but which, she had to admit, was a necessity.

A Gulf breeze made the afternoon pleasant despite the strong subtropical sun heating Annalise's back through her roomy, short-sleeved T-shirt. Thankfully, she'd slathered her arms and legs with sunblock before donning her shorts and sandals so she had no worries about her pale skin turning pink. Not a good example for a doctor to set when she warned others about avoiding sunburn.

"Need some help with those, Doc?" A bartender named Brandy pointed to the cases. Brandy sported a new tattoo, still red and slightly swollen.

Annalise hoped she'd had it done by a reputable shop. Illegal backroom bargains had consequences. She had long-lasting firsthand knowledge of that. If only hers had been as harmless as a tattoo.

"I've got them. Thanks, though." She moved forward another six inches in the queue, wincing as the corner of the cart dug into her ankle.

"Have a nice time on shore?" Bartenders were chatty by nature and Brandy was no exception.

Annalise had never learned the art of making

small talk herself, beyond the few stock phrases she used to put her patients at ease.

"Just long enough to realize I'm ready to be back at sea."

Being on land in her home port of New Orleans always made her uneasy, even though all personal threats had long since passed.

"Didn't I see you with a friend on the patio at the Crescent City Brew House this afternoon? A male friend?"

"He was my study partner in medical school." They'd been more than study partners, but the bartender didn't need to know how he'd helped her work through her pain and grief all those years ago. "He's my *platonic* friend."

"Nothing more? Not even a friend with benefits?"

Annalise laughed, inwardly wincing as it sounded brittle and forced in her ears. "He's not my type." Not that she had a type.

"What kind of man do you like, Doc? I'll bet I can fix you up. I'm fairly good at that sort of thing."

Annalise wished it were that easy. "You bartenders are really cupids in disguise, aren't you? But there are rules against that sort of thing, remember?"

"I don't know about you, Doc, but the rule against fraternization gets old when I've been out to sea for a while. It's not natural to go without sex for such long periods of time."

Sex. Shipboard sex meant a shipboard relationship—or at least a shipboard flirtation. No way would she risk her career—or her peace of mind—for a fling.

To forestall the conversation, Annalise pulled the brim of her baseball cap down tight and deliberately looked up.

From where she stood, halfway up the ship's side with the ocean far below her and the top deck far above, Annalise felt the weight of such a huge amount of people, both guests and staff, dependent upon the ship's medical facilities. As usual, she was the sole physician on board, but she had plenty of trained medical professionals to help her, including a new physician's assistant. The P.A. came with great recommendations and Annalise was looking forward to meeting her.

Her only worry was the six-year-old girl on the manifest, Sophie Christopoulos, diagnosed with juvenile diabetes. But her parents had been wise enough to have the girl's endocrinologist consult with Annalise ahead of time and Sophie had an introductory appointment before tonight's first supper seating.

Sophie's insulin was in one of the cases on her cart. With precautions, the young girl should be able to enjoy her trip just fine.

A crepe paper streamer sailed down from the top deck to drape itself across Annalise's shoulders like a boa. The makeshift fashion statement made her smile.

She looked up to see passengers on the foredeck already in full party mode and they hadn't even left dock yet. Cruises had attitudes and she could already tell this one was going to be a wild one. No peaceful, relaxing vibes coming from this crowd.

Brandy looked up, shading her eyes. "It's going to be one of those."

"The kind of cruise I enjoy most." While Annalise didn't partake of the party life herself, she enjoyed the energy.

"As long as they tip well." Brandy pointed to the sky. "Looks like a storm is coming in."

Annalise shrugged. "Typical late afternoon for New Orleans this time of year. It will blow through as fast as it's blowing in."

A thick bank of stormclouds dimmed the sun's brightness while a strong gust of wind brought chill bumps to her exposed legs. Sprigs of reddish-golden hair whipped into her face despite the baseball cap she'd plopped onto her head.

The layered cut had been a whim while she'd been on shore, a consolation prize after visiting her mother and finding her the same.

She'd thought short hair would be easier, but she missed the straightforward care of her ponytail. Now her hair was too short to capture with a rubber band and too long to stay out of her eyes without a lot of styling and primping. And primping had no place in Annalise's life. Why waste the time?

Her life was devoted to patching up people and keeping them healthy so they could enjoy their days under the sun. Stolen time away from the workaday world was precious and she wanted the passengers to be able to make the most of it.

Annalise knew the value of escaping the real world. That's why being the *Fantasy*'s onboard physician was her dream job.

A squeal of tires from the parking lot down below caught her attention.

A sporty black convertible with the top down slid into an empty parking slot and careened to a stop. Annalise squinted to see the dark-haired man behind the sunglasses pop his trunk, grab a suit-sized carry-on, a serious backpack and a large rolling suitcase and make a sprint for the entrance of the cruise ship's land-based check-in facility.

She glanced at her watch. A quarter till five.

When the cruise line said to embark before four o'clock, they had their reasons—security checks being one of the most important ones.

Brandy shook her head. "There's always one who thinks the rules don't apply to him, isn't there?"

Annalise agreed. "He'll have to do some real sweet-talking to get aboard this ship."

Brandy gazed absently at the head of the line. "Some men are worth breaking the rules for."

Not any man she'd ever met.

Stormclouds moved into position overhead, blocking the sun's intensity but adding a couple of points to the humidity scale, making the moist air heavy to drag into her lungs.

The sooner she was out at sea, the better.

"Next," came the call from the front of the line.

As she moved forward, Annalise looked back at the dark-haired latecomer juggling his luggage to open the door to the check-in office.

She had to admit he had a face and body that could entice a saint to at least bend the rules a little.

He flashed a dimpled smile at her as he caught her staring.

She could feel a blush heating her face as she looked away.

She was no saint, but the man didn't exist who could tempt her. Sadly, she wished there were.

Dr. Niko Christopoulos leaned over the counter past the plastic *Closed* sign, giving the middle-aged receptionist a big dimpled smile. He hoped she liked the rugged, unshaven look. It couldn't be helped.

"I'm so sorry to be such a bother. I've been traveling for the last thirty-two hours straight to get here and my last flight landed late."

The receptionist, who reminded him of his Aunt Phyllis with her polite but no-nonsense attitude, pulled up his information.

"You're responsible for the party of twelve, right? The grandmother who thinks she's won the family cruise?"

Niko gave a quick look around the deserted lobby, as if any of his family might overhear. "That's right. Do you need to verify my credit card?"

"We've already done that. But I do need your passport, please." She held out her hand.

He handed her the well-worn leather folder.

"The Congo, Doctor? And before that Haiti? You're quite a world traveler."

Niko didn't talk about his charity work—ever. But if it got him on this blasted ship before it sailed… "Doctors Without Borders. An adventure every trip."

Her eyes softened and she picked up the phone. "Hold the ship for Dr. Nikos Christopoulos. He was unavoidably delayed and will be heading your way in just a moment."

"Thanks for waiting on me."

She gave him a sly wink. "I'm sure you're worth waiting for."

He returned the wink. "That's what they tell me."

"Do you need help with your bags?"

"Got it all here." He pointed to his military-sized backpack full of shorts and swim trunks and toiletries, his suit bag with his tuxedo and his one rolling bag, glad he'd packed for this trip and stuffed his clothes in his trunk before he'd even left for Haiti, for once planning ahead.

He was more of a go-with-the-flow kind of guy—which came in handy when making split-second decisions in the field. Life or death decisions were enough to worry about without adding the little things to the list. But this week he intended to surrender all decisions and worries and soak in the sunshine.

He needed these three weeks of enforced restful

playtime. He had become soul-weary, the kind of tired a good nap couldn't cure.

Physician, heal thyself. He self-prescribed a big dose of fun and he intended to follow doctor's orders.

"Have a wonderful vacation, Dr. Christopoulos."

"I'll do my best." It worked. The charm his grandmother loved him for and his brothers taunted him about had gotten him where he needed to be once again.

Use the gifts you've been given, his grandmother told all of them. His brothers could all cook meals that would please the gods of Olympus. Niko couldn't boil an egg.

An easy way with words and a genetically pleasing appearance had been his gift—he just wondered if a woman would ever care enough to see past the exterior to the man underneath.

But then again, that would mean he would also need to look beneath her surface and that would mean getting up close and personal. A relationship was out of the question with the lifestyle he would soon be living full time. His ex-fiancée had made that perfectly clear to him. But that was yesterday's problem.

He would embrace today. Too many years ago

he'd learned the hard way that that's all anyone could really expect to have.

As he headed up the gangplank, the calypso music put a kick in his step. This trip may have originally been planned for his family's benefit, but it was exactly what he needed, too.

Niko breathed in the tangy air and prepared to enjoy himself, no holds barred. And maybe he'd start with that cute little honey-haired woman in the baseball cap with the legs that went on forever. She stood at the end of the line apart from everyone else, looking totally unattached, which meant totally available, right? While long-term relationships were out, shipboard flirtations were definitely in.

"Those are mighty big bags for such a little lady. Prepared to dress for dinner, are we?" Niko jiggled his suit bag for emphasis.

Big drops started to fall from the clouds above. He moved closer to squeeze under the canvas canopy sheltering the ship's entrance.

The long-legged beauty tried to shift away but there was nowhere to go.

Just as Niko was considering stepping out into the rain to put her at ease, the line moved, giving her the space she obviously needed.

Then again, it seemed this woman claimed her

own space. She looked down her nose at him as best she could, considering she was several inches shorter than him. "I'm on staff here. I don't do dinner."

Which wasn't quite true. Annalise helped out by rounding out the captain's table on occasion to even out the couples ratio. It was no hardship. Seated next to a partnerless passenger, usually an elderly gentleman or an awkward geek, she'd met some delightful people.

People like this stunning man next to her always had a date, or found one or two while shipboard. The ship's relationship rules definitely didn't apply to passengers like it did to crew.

Since she was a rule-abiding crew member, this man was not a threat. Even so, she found herself leaning away from him and his overpowering personality, even while she regretted the sharpness of her tone. She was definitely too much on edge today.

Brandy reached across her toward the guy with an open hand. "Hi, I'm—"

"Next," the security checker interrupted. He slid Brandy's ship's ID through the scanner. "You know the drill."

The tension between the security checker and

Brandy crackled, proof that shipboard break-ups made for an incredibly uncomfortable environment.

Brandy turned to Annalise. "You know, Doc, this ship is large enough that a person could sail for a month without running into everyone on board. But no matter how big it is, when you're trying to avoid someone, no ship is big enough."

Annalise felt trapped, literally being caught between a man and a woman and their conflict. A clammy sweat started down her back as the old terror threatened to overcome her.

"Relationships. Not my thing," she managed to choke out as her throat tightened up on her. She tried to laugh but it sounded strained even to her own ears so she coughed to cover it up. From bad to worse.

Behind her, the late passenger took a step forward, concern in his eyes. "Are you okay?"

His voice was a low deep rumble. Masculinity personified.

She could feel the heat from his body as he crowded her.

Annalise took a deep breath as the unreasonable panic settled. It had been a few years, almost a decade, since she'd had a panic attack. But too many memories in too few hours had taken their toll on the solid, secure world she'd built for herself.

The sooner she put New Orleans behind her, the better off she would be.

"I'm fine. Thanks." She gave a numb nod and thrust her card at the security checker, careful to keep her fingers from brushing his.

The security checker took Annalise's card and slid it through. "Welcome back, Dr. Walcott. Need some help with that load?"

"Got it. Thanks."

The man behind her held his card out for inspection.

"Could you remove the sunglasses, sir?" the security checker asked.

"Of course."

Annalise had the strongest urge to turn around so she could look into his eyes but practicality took over. What she saw there would have no bearing upon her.

As she tugged her cart, it turned sideways, crashing into this man who made her feel things she didn't want to feel.

If she were only as graceful as she was independent. "Sorry." She meant for her gaze to skitter across his face but his eyes ensnared hers.

Tiger eyes. Amber golden with specks of brown,

rimmed in a darker brown. Tiger eyes with a depth of…sorrow, perhaps, behind the brightness.

"No problem." He blinked, breaking their gaze and allowing her to blink as well. When he raised an eyebrow at her, she realized she'd been staring.

Flustered, she yanked her cart, banging into the counter and almost taking out the passenger scanner. He must think her a total klutz.

What did it matter what he thought? Odds were they would never see each other again unless he had a medical emergency. And he certainly looked healthy to her. Well-worn jeans and a wrinkled T-shirt couldn't hide his physical fitness.

She bumped into passengers all the time. None of them elicited a significant response from her.

Annalise overcame the impulse to check him out one more time.

What was it about him that made her feel… What? Aware? Self-conscious? Tingly? That made her feel anything at all?

As she fought the cart into submission, she heard the security checker say, "Welcome aboard, Mr. Christopoulos. Passenger stairway is to your left."

Christopoulos? That was the name of her patient with juvenile diabetes. What were the odds?

Annalise headed toward the staff elevators,

grateful for the privacy and breathing room that safe little metal box promised.

"Hold the door, please." A large tanned hand inserted itself between the closing doors. If the man had seemed to tower over her before, he loomed now. "You don't mind if I ride up with you, do you?"

"Passengers are encouraged to take the stairs if they're able." Inwardly, she winced at her brusqueness. She had wanted to establish distance, not convey rudeness. Where was her balance?

"I'm nursing a leg injury." He gave her a lopsided grin, as if he were embarrassed to ask for special treatment.

Annalise wished a hole would open up and swallow her. "Of course, then."

She stared at the floor numbers as the door closed, not trusting herself to engage in polite conversation.

She needn't have worried about the man being chatty. He leaned against the back wall of the elevator, closed his eyes and slumped as if he would fall asleep right then and there. Except there was nothing relaxed in the tightness around his eyes or the brackets around his mouth or the squareness of his jaw.

Annalise took a moment to gather herself the

way she'd learned in therapy so many years ago, rationalizing that her edginess had been provoked by too many triggers in quick succession, the worst one brought on by her own need to know that someone in the world cared.

When she'd knocked on her mother's apartment door while she'd been on shore leave, Annalise had half expected, even hoped, to be told that her mother had moved and failed to leave a forwarding address.

But she'd been there. Bright pink lipstick had leaked into the pursed lines around her lips and coated the end of the cigarette stuck into her mouth. Age spots showed on her chest and arms, exposed by her cheap orange tank top.

"Anna?" her mother had smoothed down her over-processed hair. "I hadn't expected…"

Scented candles perfumed the air. Annalise recognized the odor. Her mother had always thought men were turned on by heavy oriental scents. The smell made her stomach turn.

"I was in town and just thought I'd drop by."

The furtive look her mother sent over her shoulder to whoever was waiting in the back bedroom was less than welcoming.

"I don't really have the time to come in and visit," Annalise assured her.

The relief was obvious in her mother's eyes. "Maybe another time."

Her mother had closed the door between them without saying goodbye.

It had been over two years. What was another couple of years between family?

Being in her home city, seeing her mother in the old apartment she herself had once lived in, consulting with the little girl's doctor in the same building where she'd attended those therapy sessions, and then meeting with her friend had been a bit much for one day.

And this man next to her, this man who exuded power and testosterone, this man who she was too aware of being just inches away from her, had her all off balance. Something was different about him.

The elevator bumped, threatening Niko's balance. He shifted his weight. From beneath his half-closed lids, he watched Dr. Walcott do the same.

Something was different about her, something that intrigued him. An air? An attitude? A challenge?

Only problem was, Dr. Walcott didn't seem interested. Could he change her mind? When had he last been challenged?

He rubbed his hand across his heavily stubbled face.

When he saw her eyeing him, he said rather self-consciously, "This boat has plenty of hot water, right?"

"The only reason you'll take a cold shower on-board this *ship* is because you take one voluntarily."

"I don't see that happening." He flashed his dimple.

She responded with the slightest of tight-lipped curves at the corners of her mouth. Polite, but just barely.

So much for winning her over with his innate charm. But, then, he wasn't at his best.

A shower and shave and maybe a nap first. Then he might seek out the good doctor on the grounds of professional curiosity. She'd give him a tour of the facilities. He'd buy her a drink. They'd have a private meal on his room's veranda and watch the sunset together—and maybe the sunrise, too.

"How is room service?"

"Very serviceable." She bit her lower lip then squared her shoulders and took a breath as if she were about to plunge into the deep end of the pool. "I use room service quite a bit. They are very prompt. You should try the salmon mousse."

"And maybe a bottle of pinot grigio to share

with a new friend?" With the shipboard doctor, he wouldn't have to worry about expectations and entanglements.

"I've never tried it that way. But, then, I'm not very good at sharing." She glanced down at his bare finger. "I'm sure your girlfriend would enjoy the romantic gesture, though."

"No girlfriend at the moment."

She nodded her acknowledgement while she adjusted her grip on her cart, pulling it more decisively between them.

He'd gone too far, too fast. Message received.

He leaned back and closed his eyes, giving them both space.

He might be a romantic but he was a lousy long-term lover.

His ex-fiancée would be glad to expound upon that.

Impatient by nature, Niko had known there was some deep-seated, instinctive reason he'd never agreed to a wedding date. When she'd insisted he choose, either her or his work, he'd finally understood what that reason was.

Any woman who couldn't love him for who he was didn't love him at all. Sadly, after they'd both said their goodbyes, he'd realized he hadn't loved her either. He'd just thought he should because his family had insisted they were the perfect couple. And his family always knew what was best for him.

When it should have been a tragedy, breaking off their engagement had been a relief. It had also been the last tie to living the 'normal' life his family wanted him to live.

This trip was his parting gift, his apology for letting them down, his peace offering for following his dream when he knew that was the last thing any of them would want him to do.

But his lifestyle change was tomorrow's problem. Let tomorrow take care of itself.

The elevator jolted to a stop, putting the brakes on Niko's runaway thoughts.

"Your floor?"

Annalise jerked as his voice called her back to the present. She'd gone away in her mind to avoid an awkward situation as she had so often in the past. But she'd never let down her guard like that while in a confined space with a man.

He was still leaning against the wall, but one eye was cocked open. How long had the elevator been stopped with the doors gaping open?

Keep it together, Annalise. With that admonishment, Annalise pulled the tatters of her self-discipline around her, took a deep breath and determined to carry on. She gave him a sheepish smile. "Lost in thought."

"Been there, done that myself." He pushed away from the wall.

She tugged her heavy cart to get the rollers moving over the rough separation between the elevator and the hallway floor.

"Need some help?"

"No. I've got it under control." She was making more of this chance encounter than it really was, wasn't she? No man like that would be interested in a woman like her, would he?

"I'll be seeing you around."

Not if I can avoid it. She wasn't ready. Not now, maybe not ever, to feel an attraction to a man, especially a man as virile as this one.

"Enjoy your cruise."

He raised a suggestive eyebrow. "I already am."

She ignored the shiver that went through her. As she pulled her heavy load toward her clinic, she worked hard at dismissing the man who would forget about her the second the elevator doors blocked her from his sight.

Christopolous. If he was connected to her young patient, she knew all about how to keep her professional self apart from her personal self. *But was that what she really wanted?*

What she wanted was to have a normal reaction to a normal situation.

She couldn't help taking a look back.

He was watching her, appreciation on his face. He gave her a long, slow, deliberate wink.

Almost against her will her mouth quirked up at the corners, acknowledging—and enjoying?—his attention.

As she felt the ship's engines begin to churn far below her, she felt confused. She'd thought she was on an even keel, that nothing and no one could ever rock her boat.

Obviously, she'd been wrong.

Her little half-smile was more intriguing than the Mona Lisa's.

She was perfect. A woman in her profession would understand that any romance Niko allowed himself to indulge in would end when the ship docked.

Niko watched the good doctor walk away on her long, strong legs until the elevator doors closed, blocking her from view. This trip was supposed to be about family, about paying back all the sacrifices they'd made for him—even if they'd never know that part of it. But surely he'd find time for himself, time for a harmless shipboard flirtation, wouldn't he?

And if the good doctor wasn't interested, there were plenty more fish in the sea, right?

A wave of exhaustion overcame him. His long hours and primitive living conditions must be to blame. That sinking feeling certainly couldn't have come from the thought of possible rejection. His ego wasn't that big, was it?

If so, his brothers would soon set it to rights.

Niko opened the door to his home away from home for the next three weeks. While not a huge cabin, it was certainly bigger than the tent he'd been sharing with a nurse and an anesthetist for the last month.

The private veranda was big enough to dine on—and do other things on, too. Yes, this cabin would do just fine.

The quick shower he took refreshed his energy as well as his attitude. The restorative powers of hot water and a bar of soap were nothing short of miraculous. Fresh underwear was a close second.

He picked out the least wrinkled casual dress shirt and pants from his rolling bag, shaking out the mustiness. Not too bad. Packing was a skill he'd had a lot of practice with.

From the connecting door he heard a hesitant knock.

"Uncle Niko, is that you?"

"Yes, Sophie, it's me."

He finished with the last of his shirt buttons then unlatched and opened the door between them and immediately gathered up an armful of six-year-old girl. Her bouncy black curls smelled of baby shampoo and her breath smelled of sugar and spice. Too much sweetness? A hint of fruitiness? Juvenile diabetes sucked.

"Sophie, when was the last time you checked your blood sugar?"

Before Sophie could answer, a voice worn with age but sharp nevertheless, said, "What? Not even a hello first, grandson?"

He looked past Sophie, snuggled on his shoulder, to the four-foot-ten-inch paragon who ruled the Christopoulos family with an iron skillet in one hand and baklava in the other.

"Hello, Yiayia." He put down Sophie and bent to give a hug to the one woman who had always been there for him. "I've missed you."

"There's a way to prevent that. No one is making you stay away." Despite her prickly words, her hug was warm and comforting. She took a step back to look up into his face, keeping both her gnarled hands on his arms as if she could hold him in place. "Wanderlust, like your uncle and your grandfather. At least you have sense enough to keep yourself from getting killed. If I hadn't won this trip, I don't know when we would have seen you next."

Niko squirmed inside while he kept his smile brightly in place. "Livin' the dream, Yiayia."

His mercy missions meant everything to him. But his family would not be pleased if they knew he put himself in such danger, risking his life in areas where lives were lost in wars over water wells as frequently as they were from malaria. His thigh throbbed in memory.

The life of a an overworked, barely paid medical relief doctor was not the life his family had envisioned for him as they'd all sacrificed to send him to college and on to medical school.

He owed them so much. Could he do it? Could he follow his passion, leaving his family with loans and bills and kids to put through college—like they'd put him through all those years.

Yiayia pointed her bony finger at him. "The Christopoulos men are all lucky in love. Someday soon you will find the perfect woman and give me beautiful great-grandbabies."

"Maybe someday, Yiayia." It was easier to agree

with her than to argue. And he certainly didn't want to start off a three week vacation on her bad side.

He was so unlike his three brothers in so many ways. Not being cut out to be a family man was the one that hurt the most. He'd dated his fair share of women and then some but he'd not found one he wanted to spend a week with, much less a lifetime.

He flashed the smile that always worked with her. "You've set my standards too high, Yiayia. No other woman can compare."

Yiayia reached up and pinched his cheek. "How can I stay mad at a face like this?"

Sophie had waited as long as she could. She jumped up and down to get attention. "I'm hungry. Ice cream, Yiayia! Ice cream!"

Yiayia's eyes sparkled as bright as Sophie's. "It's included in the trip, Niko. Did they tell you that? Any time we want some. And fine dining each evening, too. Such a dream come true."

It felt good to give back to the family that had sacrificed so much to give him his dream. They would have never accepted repayment for all the support they'd given him through the years. And they all certainly needed a break after the year and a half they'd just been through. If only he hadn't had to set up such an elaborate ruse…

"All right, little one. Let me get my room key." Yiayia turned to find the key.

Niko stopped his grandmother with a gentle hand on her arm. "Wait, Yiayia. What's Sophie's blood-sugar level?"

Yiayia had always made her little ones feel better through food and didn't understand why it had to be different with Sophie—which was one of the main reasons why Niko had agreed to oversee Sophie's care while onboard ship. All his brothers concurred that he had a way with Yiayia that none of the other three had.

"How do I know, Niko? You're the doctor in the family." She switched to Greek, a language Niko heard rarely and only among his grandmother's contemporaries who had immigrated to the United States when she had. But he understood the gist of it.

Yiayia was resistant to taking the disciplined stance needed to protect Sophie's health, thinking everyone was blowing it all out of proportion when her great-granddaughter looked just fine to her.

Niko gave her a stern look. "Where's her blood-glucose meter?"

"In my luggage. I haven't had a chance to unpack yet. She has to check in with the ship's doctor thirty minutes before supper, anyway."

Niko glanced down at Sophie, who was looking scared behind that pout she was sporting. The kid had been through even more than the rest of them.

In addition to being diagnosed with juvenile diabetes, her mother had lost a baby and almost her life through miscarriage when their restaurant had had the kitchen fire. All the trauma had been straining a marriage that had been made in heaven. Sophie's home life had been tense day in and day out for a long time.

The only reason Niko's oldest brother and sister-in-law had let their daughter come without them was because they were on the verge of emotional exhaustion and Sophie's doctor had insisted it would be better for Sophie to be away from the stress and tension for a while. So they had stayed behind to keep the restaurant open and work on their relationship, knowing Sophie would be surrounded by aunts, uncles, cousins and Yiayia, who would all watch out for her.

"I'll take her, Yiayia." He checked his watch. "We're a bit early but we'll stop in and say hello to the doctor while you look for that meter."

He'd promised his brother he would take care of Sophie. Who could have known his solemn vow would have the side benefit of bringing him together with the good doctor? Niko knew enough about life to make use of good luck when it presented itself.

And now he intended to take full advantage.

CHAPTER TWO

ONCE SAFELY IN her medical suite, Annalise took a deep breath, the first one she'd managed since that man had crowded her in the line boarding the ship.

Surrounded by the tools of her trade, she found her inner balance. If she could relive those brief moments as she boarded the ship…

But, then, going back in time wasn't possible, no matter how hard she wished for it.

She dragged her clunking cases in front of the locked refrigerator reserved for medicines and inserted her key.

As Annalise put away the supplies she'd brought on board, bumping the bottles and boxes into uniform rows, she felt calm claim her. She pushed away the sheepishness she felt about overreacting. Emotional incidents happened on occasion, especially after such a trying day. Being ashamed of her reaction did nothing but undermine her success in coping.

The bell chimed, signaling someone had come

into the medical suite. Officially, office hours didn't start until tomorrow morning, but she had scheduled a visit with her juvenile diabetes patient to make sure they started off on the right foot. She glanced at her watch. Better early than late.

"But I don't want to get stuck, Uncle Niko."

Annalise heard them before she saw them as they entered the anteroom of the medical suite.

"Can't be helped, Sophie."

Sophie—it was the Christopoulos child.

That was his voice, wasn't it? The elevator guy was with her little patient. Sometimes luck wasn't in her favor.

Still, she liked it that he didn't trivialize Sophie's fears.

She'd checked the manifest earlier—solely to see where her little patient's cabin would be and to verify that a small refrigerator had been moved into her cabin. She found it had been moved to the cabin next door, Niko Christopoulos' room.

The girl was staying in the cabin next door to the refrigerator with her great-grandmother, Olympia Christopoulos. Twelve people surnamed Christo-poulos, all with adjoining cabins or family suites, were on the ship, which had made the odds good she might run into him again.

She thought she'd braced herself for that strange

feeling he'd caused in her. But her stomach gave a little flutter, knowing she'd soon be face to face with him again.

Apprehension? More than that.

Fear?

No. Not fear.

Anticipation, maybe?

Before she could sort that one out in her mind she rounded the corner and realized she'd down-played his good looks in her mind. How could a real flesh-and-blood man be put together so well without magazine airbrushing to lend a hand?

He'd changed. He wore a charcoal-gray boxy button-down made of a silky cotton so fine it slid over his chest when he moved. Even though she wasn't the touchy-feely type, she wanted to rub it between her fingers—purely for curiosity's sake. And his white linen slacks looked loose, comfortable, deceptive. She remembered the shape of him in those jeans.

As he filled her office suite, she felt as if an electric current rode just below the surface of her skin. Unsettling was an understatement. But also energizing? Good? Bad?

She wasn't sure.

Annalise stood a bit taller and smoothed down the lab coat she'd thrown over the chocolate-brown tailored slacks and matching loose blouse she'd changed into.

She felt acutely aware of herself as a woman, an awareness she always pushed down the list behind physician the minute she donned her lab coat.

What was happening to her?

Why now? Why him—okay, that one was easy. How could any woman not fail to go into immediate estrogen overload with him in such close proximity?

He held a notebook. The masculinity of his hand contrasted drastically with the notebook cover, which was totally overlaid with pink glittery stickers.

"Hi, again." He stuck out his free right hand. "Niko Christopoulos, and this is my niece, Sophie."

Sophie wore a baby-blue sailor dress with a large white collar and red cowgirl boots. Annalise could imagine the conversation between this little girl with the adorable stubborn jaw and the person who had helped her dress.

She took Niko's hand, long-fingered and large enough to engulf hers, and that fluttery feeling intensified to an erratic quivering that grew as the seconds ticked by.

Using all her willpower, she made herself hold tight when she wanted to jerk back.

Then he quirked his eyebrow and glanced at their bonded hands.

How was she going to handle this?

Her fallback answer. Professionalism.

She released his hand and used her best patient care smile she'd practiced so hard to perfect. "Welcome, Sophie. I'm Dr. Walcott."

"Uncle Niko is a doctor, too."

"Really?" That didn't surprise her. With his composure, Annalise was sure Niko Christopoulos could be anything he wanted to be.

Annalise squatted down to eye level with her patient, which gave her a good view of Niko Christopoulos' expensive shoes. "And what do you want to be when you grow up?"

"A cook, of course. That's what we all are—except for Uncle Niko." She said it as if becoming a doctor instead of a cook was the most rebellious thing a man could do.

Niko shifted, causing Annalise to look up.

His eyes were tense and his mouth bracketed at the corners. "That's not true, Sophie. Your mother is studying to become a nurse."

"And my dad says it's all your fault."

He gave a deep, sad sigh as he held out his hand

to help Annalise stand. "Maybe I should start over. Niko Christopoulos, black sheep of the family."

Annalise wanted to make up an excuse to ignore his outstretched hand, but she couldn't bring herself to reject the man even that small bit when he'd obviously been rejected enough by his own family. She knew how that felt.

"Dr. Christopoulos, it's a pleasure to meet you." As she said the niceties, he wrapped his hand around hers again, this time with the slightest of familiar pressure as if they were comrades in arms. Between his strength and his warmth she felt cocooned. Before she could feel trapped, he released her.

"Call me Niko. Professional courtesy, right? And you are…?"

She was a woman who rarely gave out her first name to strangers, liking the barrier titles and surnames erected around her.

"Annalise." Saying her own name aloud felt so intimate, like a secret revealed. Trying to erase the uneasy feeling, she said in her most authoritative voice, "I understand you're in charge of your niece's blood-sugar checks while you're aboard. Do you understand how to balance her food and activity with her insulin? Are you comfortable giving injections? I can give you a refresher course if you like. I know some doctors don't give injections regularly."

"Got it down." His sister-in-law had emailed Sophie's requirements and he had studied them on the plane.

"I don't want a shot. I don't like Uncle Niko being a doctor."

Annalise shouldn't get involved in family relations but she found herself saying, "I think it's awesome your Uncle Niko is a doctor. He helps people feel better."

"Daddy says Uncle Niko makes people's noses smaller and his wallet bigger."

This time Niko grinned, his cat eyes sparkling. "Guilty." He gave Annalise a wink. "Although I can see my services are not needed here as you have a perfect nose. But we need your professional help, Dr. Walcott. We need to check Sophie's blood sugar."

Annalise had a huge moment of doubt. "You don't know how to use her meter?"

Sophie looked down at her red boots. "Yiayia might have forgotten my blood-sugar meter in the car."

Niko kept his smile firmly in place to hide his disappointment with Yiayia. She couldn't seem to understand how important it was to monitor Sophie's condition. Juvenile diabetes could get out of hand in a heartbeat.

"It's hard for some family members to accept their young ones needing such continuous care," Annalise said sympathetically.

Apparently, she saw behind his smile. He must be slipping. He *was* beyond tired. Could he catch a nap on deck after supper? A few moments of solitude would go a long way to preparing him to facing three weeks with his raucous family *en masse*.

Annalise pulled up Sophie's charts on her computer screen. "When's the last time you ate, Sophie?"

Sophie shrugged, uncharacteristically shy, and pointed to the notebook her uncle held.

Niko turned to the last entry and angled it so Annalise could have a look at the meal listed there. Fast food at a burger joint. There were better choices—much better.

Sophie was young, but she would still have to be taught to be aware of what she ate.

Annalise asked in a different way. "What did you have for lunch?"

"French fries."

"Anything else?" Niko prompted.

"Aunt Phoebe made me eat my hamburger meat,

but I didn't want to and Yiayia said I shouldn't have to because we were on vacation."

"Aunt Phoebe did the right thing." Annalise opened a cabinet and brought out a glucose meter. "Ready?"

Sophie folded her hands together behind her back and stuck out her chin. "No."

Niko's heart broke for her. Life wasn't fair.

What method of persuasion would work best with her?

Of all his nieces and nephews, Sophie was the most stubborn of the bunch. She'd often been compared to him. What would have worked best for him?

"Sophie Olympia Christopoulos, I'm not going to treat you like a baby. You're too brave for that. Now stick that finger out there and prove it to me."

Niko could see the wheels turning in Sophie's little brain and knew he'd scored. She stood up straighter and held out a finger. Right before Annalise rested the meter against it, Sophie broke. "Hold my hand, Uncle Niko, so it won't go and hide again."

Niko looked up at the ceiling, trying to find the strength before looping his fingers firmly around her tiny wrist. "All right. Let's do this."

"Are you ready?" Annalise moved quickly, pricking in mid-sentence before Sophie had a chance to tense up more. "It's over."

Sophie looked surprised. "That's it?"

"That's it."

"When Daddy does it, it hurts more."

Niko could guess why. His brother probably let the drama build so high that the fear was worse than the prick.

It seemed a family meeting was in order.

The tug o'war that had been pulling at him all these months gave a jerk to his gut. He was the doctor in the family, the one they'd all sacrificed to put through medical school. The one they relied on for explaining these kinds of things. But he'd been out of town and out of touch more often than not.

And, if all went as planned, after this trip, he would be practically unreachable most of the time.

Guilt bowed his shoulders.

Annalise read the numbers then showed them to Niko. He hid his wince then checked his watch.

"We'll eat in fifteen minutes. It's about time for insulin, rapid and long-acting. Let's go with the same amount and I'll make sure she eats better this meal to balance it out."

"Sounds good. Check again a few hours before bedtime to see if she needs a snack. Ask your waiter to bring apples and orange juice to keep in your room's refrigerator."

"Will do."

"Ice cream!" Sophie said. "I want ice cream. Yiayia said I could have—"

Niko cocked his eyebrow, stopping her whine in mid-sentence. "If you eat your meal, you can have a little for dessert."

While Annalise opened up her refrigerator and took out a vial of insulin, Niko paged through the notebook. "Abdomen for breakfast and lunch, thigh for supper, right?"

Annalise double-checked her notes. "Yes. And today is left side, tomorrow is right side."

Sophie's face clouded up as tears formed in the corners of her eyes. She looked so small and delicate.

Niko felt so powerless. Injections and a strict regimen were Sophie's fate for the rest of her life.

He picked her up to sit her on the examining table, giving her a big hug midway. "Sweetie, I would take this for you if I could, but I can't."

"If I don't eat, I don't have to have a shot, right?"

"Not an option, little one."

He took the vials from Annalise and filled the syringe to the proper marking.

"Hold your finger out like a candle, sweetie." He held up his own finger, showing her.

"I'm going to hold your leg still." He put his hand on her thigh. "When I say, 'Now,' pretend you're blowing out the candle. Be sure to blow hard."

She gave him a confused look.

"Trust me." He focused on the injection site. "Now."

While Sophie blew, Niko took advantage of her distraction and injected the insulin.

"Good girl. All over." He jotted down the particulars in Sophie's notebook, taking a moment to appreciate the details his brothers and sisters-in-law were trying so carefully to document.

"You want to dig through the treasure chest, Sophie, and pick out a toy?"

"Okay." Sophie shrugged, not looking very excited. After all these months of doctors' visits she'd probably been rewarded with too many cheap toys in the past to make this one special.

Annalise helped Sophie down from the table then opened a huge plastic tub filled with monster trucks and snorkels and magic wands.

"I think there's a superhero cape in there somewhere. A real one."

Sophie began flinging plastic trucks and coloring books out of the box, digging for the cape. "Really?"

"Absolutely. I save the good stuff for the most courageous girls and boys."

Niko gave Dr. Annalise Walcott a long look. She was a smart one, reinforcing Niko's challenge to be brave with an enticing reward. Small things made big impressions with little patients. While he had the minimum of pediatrics training, he'd treated enough frightened children to pick up a thing or two. Apparently, Annalise had treated her own fair share of children, too.

"Found it!" Sophie triumphantly held up a bright pink cape along with the sparkling wand attached to it.

Niko quickly yanked off and crumpled up the tag that declared it a fairy costume instead of a superheroine disguise.

As she pointed the wand at him, he obligingly shrank back with as much mock terror on his face as he could muster. "SuperSophie. If I were a nasty villain, I would be quaking in my shoes right now."

"Let me tie it on for you," Annalise offered.

The pleased smile she gave Sophie made Niko think the good doctor really had picked out the cape herself. With her long legs she'd make the perfect bustiered and masked crusader.

Niko rubbed his hand over his eyes, clearing the vision. What was it about this demure doctor that had his imagination running wild? Had he been under so much pressure that he needed to resort to a fantasy life for relief? If so, what did that say for his stamina in the field?

Lack of resilience or desire to make a difference wasn't what sidelined most of the special mission doctors. Coping with the mental stress, knowing they were only making a small dent in the needs of so many was what broke most of them.

Then again, maybe Annalise brought out the creative imagination in him. Nothing wrong with that, was there? This was a fantasy cruise after all.

"You're really good with her, Dr. Christopoulos. I'm impressed." When she smiled, her gaze was honest, her voice sincere. It felt better than good to be appreciated.

"It's Niko." His own voice was huskier than normal.

"Niko." She licked her full lips.

Fascinating and, oh, so sexy with no contrivance or even an awareness of what her mouth could do to a man.

Niko reined himself in. It had been a while. Where he'd been wasn't exactly an environment conducive to lovemaking.

How did he ask the good doctor if she would like to share a drink with him under the stars tonight? How could he make himself stand out in a crowd when he bet every man on board this ship would like to do the same?

I don't do dinner, she'd said.

She'd been offputting on the gangway, but Niko could understand why. She probably had to field invitations and propositions all day, every day from total strangers.

What made him different from them? And why did it matter so much that he was? There were plenty of women aboard this ship looking for a diversion. But he had no interest in pursuing them. Only her.

What made her different?

He didn't know, but he wanted to find out.

He searched for the right pick-up line but came up blank. What was the matter with him? He'd had no trouble knowing what to say to charm the opposite sex since he'd turned twelve.

"What? Do I have something on my face?" Annalise wiped away a non-existent blemish.

"How about sharing a bottle of wine tonight?" Nothing glib or witty or clever there. Just a straightforward request. "I thought, as colleagues, we could discuss medicine aboard ship. Strictly professional curiosity."

She was shaking her head before she even started to turn him down. "I don't really think…"

That's when he heard them coming. No one could ever say a Christopoulos didn't give you fair warning before arriving. From the sound of it, the whole family was in the medical suite's anteroom.

Annalise looked alarmed.

"Not to worry. It's not a mass emergency. Just an invasion of family."

Family. Wasn't that what he'd wanted when he'd planned this elaborate ruse, to spend time with family? Why was he even trying to strike up a shipboard romance with a woman who obviously had no interest in him?

He had to admit, paying attention to a beautiful woman sounded a lot more enticing than paying attention to his brothers as they droned on about the restaurant or to the sisters-in-law as they expounded on the joys and tribulations of parenthood.

As he and Sophie joined them he realized, as he had so many times in the past, that he was a square peg in a family of round holes. Now he understood that no amount of buying anonymous vacations was going to change that.

Seeing his sisters-in-law with children in tow, he also understood that no number of casual relationships would fill that hole of not having someone special to belong to, like his brothers did.

Choices. Live every man's dream or live his own personal dream.

He would never again become involved with a woman who made him feel the pain of having to choose.

Annalise.

The good doctor was safe, right?

At a glance, Annalise recognized the people in her waiting room as family. They looked—and sounded—exactly alike.

Still, while the family resemblance was strong, Niko stood apart.

One of the lanky teenaged boys jostled another, who looked like an identical twin. "Of course we'd find Uncle Niko down here, playing doctor with the nurse."

"I'd expect you to be out by the pool, Uncle Niko, checking out the bikini babes. When we walked by, there was this one…" He raised his hands like he was holding coconuts, or maybe watermelons.

Niko cut them both a harsh look. "Respect," he growled.

At the same time as one of the women gave the twins a sharp look and said, "Boys, behave."

Amidst the chaos of the two women and smaller children throwing themselves into Niko's arms and the two men patting him on the back, Niko made introductions.

"Dr. Walcott, these are my brothers and their wives, with assorted nieces and nephews and my grandmother in the back. Family, meet Dr. Walcott. She will be helping us while we're here."

A tiny older woman, small in stature but big in presence, waded through three waist-high children and elbowed her way past the two tall boys to the front of the crowd. "I am Olympia Christopoulos. Everyone calls me Yiayia. We were all greatly relieved to learn the ship has its own doctor to help us with our little Sophie."

Surprising Annalise, Yiayia wrapped her in a big hug. Annalise flailed her arms, unsure what to do, who to be. Should she pretend to be the type of person who was comfortable with this type of thing? Should she hug back? Finally, the hug was over and Annalise could be herself again.

Too late, she wished she'd wrapped her arms around the old woman, just to see what having a grandmother might feel like.

The woman who belonged to the twin boys

turned to Niko and patted her huge Hawaiian print tote bag. "I have the meter. I see you have the notebook. It's time for Sophie's s-h-o-t."

From the stricken look on Sophie's face she clearly knew what word the woman had just spelled out.

Niko gave Sophie a reassuring pat. "Already taken care of, Phoebe."

"You wrote it all down in the notebook, right? The time and the amount and her blood-sugar reading?" She turned to Annalise. "You know how men are. They don't always think of these things."

Who were these people? They acted as if they didn't even acknowledge that Niko was a doctor in his own right. Or was that a good-natured tease? Maybe this was just a normal give and take of a normal family. Group dynamics wasn't her strong suit.

"Don't worry, sis. I learned how to chart in medical school." Despite Niko's self-deprecating smile, his tone held a hint of bite and his jaw held more than a hint of firmness.

His sister-in-law must have seen the same sparks in Niko's eyes that Annalise saw because she tried to excuse herself by saying, "Of course you did, Niko. It's just that you don't usually have children as patients and you have that big staff to do things for you."

Annalise envisioned a spa-like office suite with customized furniture arranged by a top designer, staff in matching trendy uniforms and coffee and tea with French names available to sip as the clientele discussed lifting brows, firming chins and reshaping cheekbones.

Her own utilitarian facilities would be stark in comparison. Still, her suite and her staff were top of the line, assembled to handle any emergency.

One of the men, older than Niko but definitely related, stepped forward. "Time to eat. Let's see how cruise-ship food stacks up to Christopoulos food."

A twin clapped Niko on the shoulder. "It'll be nice to be served instead of being the server for a change, too. But, then, you never had to do the waiter thing, did you, Uncle Niko?"

The tiny ancient woman reached up and tweaked the boy's ear. "If your grades were as good as Niko's, you wouldn't either."

Phoebe turned to Annalise. "Niko tutored during high school instead of working in the restaurant."

Annalise processed information, trying to fill in the holes while simultaneously wondering why this family would reveal so much to a total stranger.

"Good thing Niko's so smart since he can't cook worth a flip," the other brother added. "Now, let's go and eat."

En masse, they turned and exited, carrying Sophie along with them but leaving Niko behind.

He raised an eyebrow. "Family. Gotta love 'em, right?"

No. No, you didn't. Annalise knew that first hand. But that was knowledge she had no intention of sharing. Sharing meant intimacy and intimacy was something Annalise didn't do, especially with a man who made her breath skip when he stood this close.

She fell back on her professionalism. "Enjoy your dinner. Bring Sophie back any time you need to."

"Thanks."

Annalise stood by the glass door and watched him walk away.

It wasn't that she didn't like to look at men—she just liked to look from a distance. Now she allowed herself to admire the breadth of his shoulders and tautness of his butt even while her medical training had her noticing the slight hesitation of his left leg as he climbed the short flight of stairs leading to the main hallway. He'd said something about an injury when he boarded the elevator with her, hadn't he?

Not her concern unless he sought out medical attention. She had to remind herself of that daily when she wanted to fix the world.

When her office was empty once again, it felt as if all the energy had been sucked out with the Christopoulos family.

No, not energy. They had taken joyous chaos with them when they'd left. The energy had gone with Niko, along with the impression of stability he projected of keeping that wild bunch under control.

Usually her haven, the atmosphere of the medical suite felt as cold as the stainless steel of the countertops and she felt restless, on the verge—but on the verge of what?

Underneath her feet the rumble of the huge engines reverberated as they churned through the waters of the Gulf of Mexico on their way towards the open water of the Atlantic.

She was being silly. The feel of freedom was all around her. Why, then, was she missing the anchoring sensation Niko had taken with him?

CHAPTER THREE

NIKO SAT AT the dining table surrounded by family, knowing he'd turned down his best chance of a family of his own.

His ex-fiancée hadn't asked him for anything extraordinary—only to give up his work, to give up his soul.

She hadn't understood. He hadn't been able to make her understand what Doctors Without Borders meant to him. That he'd never felt more alive as he beat the odds, winning out over a harsh world unlike any his family had ever seen and snatching the downtrodden back from the edge of death. What were the odds he could make his family understand anyway?

Misunderstood. Different. The story of his life. Was there anyone on the planet who could understand?

In walked Annalise Walcott. She'd shed her lab coat, exposing the silk blouse over her trousers. Classy.

She was the total package, wasn't she? Brains and beauty. Such a winning combination.

While he'd appreciated the shorts earlier on the gangway, now he appreciated the way her silky blouse moved across her...

"Uncle Niko, what are you staring at?" His nephew Marcus interrupted as the teen followed Niko's line of sight.

"Just taking in the scenery."

"You mean that brunette at that corner table? She looks like your type."

Niko checked out the voluptuous dark-haired woman sitting alone. Big hair, big earrings, big bone structure, everything he usually liked in a woman. He even liked her interesting nose, more aquiline than fashionable, but it suited her. "She's okay, I guess."

Beside him, Yiayia was taking a keen interest in the conversation while trying to appear as if she wasn't.

"You're not talking about Dr. Walcott, are you?" Marcus asked.

"Absolutely."

His nephew gave him a quizzical look. "She's not Greek."

"It's not like I'm going to marry her."

Marcus laughed. "Everyone knows you're not the

marrying kind, Uncle Niko. We all live through you vicariously, even Dad." Marcus elbowed his father next to him to get his attention.

Niko's brother Stephen gave him a somber frown. "You've got to settle down sometime, Niko. We all liked Melina. Maybe if you talked to her? Apologized for whatever you did. Or even if you didn't do anything—"

"My broken engagement is none of your business, brother."

Stephen narrowed his eyes, but backed down and looked away when Niko continued to glare, using refilling his wife's wine glass as his excuse to turn away.

The eight years that separated them in age also separated them in values. Or maybe they were just too different. His brothers were so much like the father he could barely remember, while he was his own person.

If only he didn't have to keep reminding them of that.

Marcus spoke barely loud enough to hear. "It's true, isn't it, Uncle Niko? The Christopoulos men are destined to be family men, aren't they?"

"You've been listening to Yiayia too much." Niko could see a lifetime of family tradition shackling his nephew, just as it tried to shackle him.

"Every man has to find his own purpose. Family is a very good purpose—just not for everyone." Knowing what he was about to do was tantamount to anarchy, Niko leaned in and pinned his nephew with his stare. "Promise me, Marcus, that you'll take some time to think about what *you* want—not what anyone else expects from you."

Marcus swallowed hard. "Not everyone is as strong-willed as you are, Uncle Niko. I envy that about you. But someday..."

Niko thought of all the trips he took abroad with Doctors Without Borders, the trips his family thought he took for leisure. They thought he was gallivanting to tropical paradises, giving his wild side a long leash before settling down while his partners carried his load.

He encouraged them to think that. What would they think if they knew his partners admired and supported his perilous service work? And how would they feel about him if they knew family wasn't on his radar?

Not providing grandchildren was the second-biggest sin in the Christopoulos family Bible, right under "Don't live dangerously."

It was a rule he wasn't very good at following. Neither had his uncle or his grandfather. But, then, his parents had both been killed in a car wreck while on a trip to the store. Playing it safe didn't mean a person would *be* safe. And following the family rules didn't mean he would be happy like they were.

How did the good doctor juggle her family with her medical practice? Working on a cruise ship, she was separated from her loved ones more often than not, wasn't she?

Because he was staring, and because she turned and caught him at it, he stood and walked toward her to invite her over.

She looked around, as if she were looking to see who he was approaching.

He brightened up his smile a few notches.

She gave him a nervous smile back, shook her head and started to turn away. And his ego took the well-aimed shot to heart. Of all the women in all the world, why did he have to find this one so fascinating?

Then fate worked in Niko's favor. The captain, coming up behind her, helpfully pointed out that a guest was requesting her presence.

"Good evening." As the ship rocked, the captain politely rested his hand on Annalise's back, effectively keeping her still and steady. "Are you in need of our doctor?"

Niko had the strongest urge to push away the captain's hand, replacing it with his own.

Need. Yes, he was in need of her. Just standing next to her made endorphins flood his brain. What was it about her? And what excuse could he use to keep her close to him?

"If you have a few seconds, Dr. Walcott, I could use the reinforcement when I explain once again to Sophie's grandmother why Sophie can't have late-night snacks."

The captain dropped his hand and Annalise took a breath and an automatic step back from Niko, trying to find her comfort zone. But nothing about this man could be described as comfortable. As soon as the captain was out of earshot, she called him on his excuse. "I've seen you with your family, remember? When you speak, they all look at you as if every word was gold. You don't need any help from me, Doctor."

"But I do." His tiger eyes glittered. "You might notice I'm the only unmarried brother left. My family would like to change that. You'll keep me safe from their matchmaking, at least for tonight."

Too aware that everyone at Niko's table intently watched them, Annalise hesitated.

"Please?"

Annalise had never been able to turn down a plea

for help—at least, that's what she told herself as she said, "Okay. But don't make a habit of this."

As she wove in and out, past the other diners, she questioned herself but could come up with no reason why she hadn't made her usual polite escape whenever a man took notice of her.

Was it the sincerity in his voice? What about him made her feel ready to respond to the interest in a man's eyes?

All the Christopoulos men stood as Annalise approached their table. Their good manners made her feel self-conscious and very feminine.

With Sophie now cuddled in her Aunt Phoebe's lap, it left an open seat between him and Yiayia.

As Niko pulled out the chair for her, he leaned in and whispered, "You're blushing. Nice."

"I'm not used to such..." She held her hand out to the standing men, speechless.

"A show of good manners," Yiayia finished her sentence. "Take it as your due, dear. You deserve it."

What would it be like to be a part of a large family where she was loved and respected on a daily basis?

A warm glow deep inside vied with the chill of nerves prickling along her skin.

Conflicted. Was she doomed to always be conflicted?

"Wine, Doctor?" A server held the bottle of merlot for her inspection.

Normally, Annalise would say no. While she enjoyed an occasional glass of wine with a good book, she never drank in uncomfortable social situations. But she found herself saying yes instead.

"And you, sir?" the waiter asked Niko.

He started to shake his head, but his brother Stephen was nodding instead.

"Give the man another drink. He's a doctor, you know? Under stress all the time. Look at that strain around his eyes. You need to cut loose every now and then, Niko, or you'll be looking as old as me before your time." Stephen held his glass out. "And pour me another one, too, will you?"

Niko knew his brother's remark was a dig at his supposed frivolous lifestyle, which Stephen was both jealous of and proud he'd played a part in providing. Niko should have never let the misunderstanding lie between them for so long.

But so much had been happening when he'd left for his first mission. The restaurant fire, the miscarriage that had threatened his sister-in-law's life and Sophie's diagnosis had rocked the foundations of his very strong family.

Leaving his family at their time of need had been the hardest decision he'd ever had to make.

He wasn't good at raw emotion. Just being there for his loved ones had made him feel trapped and helpless—made him remember too much.

He'd had to take action. Do something. Fix something. There had been nothing he could do for his family to make them any better.

But he'd had the medical dossiers of a half-dozen children in his briefcase—children who could die without his medical care. He'd decided he would only be in the way if he stayed around.

He'd reasoned that there was no sense in adding to everyone's worries if Doctors Without Borders wasn't for him. Now that he'd made his decision, he wouldn't put a damper on this trip, but he would tell them at the end that working for Doctors Without Borders would be permanent.

He had already made arrangements to begin the sale of his share of the partnership as soon as he returned home. But for now he would keep pretending, for their sakes.

"Everything okay?" Annalise's hand fluttered over his arm, as if she wanted to touch him but felt he was off limits.

Niko pasted on his brightest smile. "I'm sharing a glass of wine with a brilliant, beautiful woman. What could be better? Except maybe a bit of privacy."

While he didn't know her well, he read her eyes with ease. Concern turned to disappointment. It seemed that's all he did lately, disappoint the women in his life.

But, then, Annalise wasn't in his life, was she? She was a simple, uncomplicated diversion. In three weeks, walking out of her life would be as easy as walking off this ship.

He'd meant to be flippant, but he tempered it with truth. "I've got a lot going on in my head right now. I guess I haven't quite made the transition to vacation mode yet."

As the waiter made the rounds, Niko held out his glass after all. "To vacations."

The rest of the family held their glasses aloft and echoed his toast before drinking.

When the server would have moved away, Yiayia stopped him, holding out her glass for a refill.

"Just leave the bottle. We'll serve ourselves." Phoebe grinned at the young waiter. "We've had practice."

As Phoebe topped up the adults' glasses, Marcus did the same with the tea and juice pitchers for the children.

"A toast. To my grandson the doctor." Everyone held their glasses high then drank. Even the children downed their glasses in style. Bewildered at first, Annalise looked around and followed suit. Niko had to smile at her quick assimilation into his crazy family. If he were looking for a woman…

But who said anything about finders keepers?

He gave her a wink before saluting the table with his glass. "To my family, who put me through college and medical school."

Annalise raised her eyebrows then drank with him as the rest of the family looked at each other, well satisfied with their sacrifice. His decision would be so much easier if they weren't so proud of him.

"And to my brother and sister-in-law who could not be with us today." Stephen, as second oldest, did the honors to acknowledge them.

As soon as Niko took the obligatory swallow, he leaned over and explained to Annalise, "Family tradition. We'll finish off the bottle this way."

As the young nephews and nieces started to droop, climbing into any available adult lap for a good cuddle, Yiayia began her bragging. "Dr. Walcott, did you know that my grandson has been on national television, on a talk show? Did you know that he operates on all the famous actors and actresses? But he won't tell us who they are. Confidentiality issues. It's all very mysterious. They bring them up through the hospital's loading dock."

"Remember that time you made your cucumber yogurt for that actress when Uncle Niko wired her jaw shut?" Phoebe turned to Annalise. "He still won't tell us her name, even though we've begged. He's very discreet is our Niko."

Under cover of their chatter, Niko said to Annalise, "You're very quiet. Don't wait for a turn to talk. Just jump in anywhere."

"I'd rather listen." She gave him a smug smile. "I'm learning a lot about you this way."

Niko was one part chagrined over his family's bragging and the other part overjoyed that Annalise wanted to know more about him.

"Then it's only fair I get to hear your life story, too."

When Annalise looked around the full table tensely, he quickly reassured her, "When we have time to ourselves. I'll want all your intimate details."

Visibly, Annalise shivered. While Niko would usually regard her reaction as a positive response in anticipation of time together, the way she held herself so tightly told him he'd overstepped the mark.

To break the tension, he refilled her glass even though she'd only been taking the tiniest of sips.

She took the glass, looking into it as if searching

for answers. "I'm not much on pillow talk." Her voice was husky, hesitant and, oh, so sexy.

She was so much more intense than the women he usually dated, like the Greek goddess in the corner, laughing loudly and holding court with the ship's captain. Annalise wasn't his usual type at all. Whatever type she was, she'd captured his interest and he couldn't seem to let go.

He would need to go slowly with her, pace himself. It was a novel concept when he usually got what he wanted when he wanted. His brothers would find this strain on his ego amusing. He himself found it challenging.

Marcus leaned over his mother to tell Annalise, "Some big charity wants to auction off a date with Uncle Niko. He did it last year and cameras followed him around all night, even when he kissed her."

Phoebe pushed her son back into place without jiggling the sleeping young nephew on her lap. "It would be good if you could bring your date back to the restaurant this year, Niko. We got a lot of publicity from that and we could certainly use it again."

He would have to tell them. No more celebrity stories. No more TV appearances. No more magazine layouts for the hottest catch in the Crescent City.

"Niko? Are you okay?" Stephen's concern brought him out of his thoughts.

He blinked, back in the game. "Fine. Just tired."

Yiayia was telling the good doctor about her own excitement in front of the media crew—a crew Niko had bought and paid for.

"And then this pretty little blonde girl handed me a huge check, just like on the television, and this man with a video camera asked how I felt." Yiayia told her sweepstakes story to Annalise. "I thought I would have a heart attack right then and there. And, of course, no doctor around."

She patted Niko on the shoulder. "My grandson is never home. Itchy feet, just like my late husband Leo. The places we would go when we were young... We travelled around the world before Leo brought me to America and that's the place that felt like home. Travelling is a good thing to do when you're young." She looked around the luxurious dining room of the cruise ship and smiled. "And good to do when you get old, too,"

That smile made all the planning, all the money and all the subterfuge worth it.

As his brother reached past him for the bread basket, doubt jabbed Niko. If he stayed with his practice, he could give his family many more trips like this one. His brothers could expand the restaurant, hire more employees, spend more time with their children.

Although he tried to stop himself, he couldn't help glancing Annalise's way. What would she think of him giving up all his family had worked so hard for on his behalf? Would she judge him to be as ungrateful as he judged himself?

‚But, then, this was a woman who called a berth on a ship home. Obviously, she was following her dream.

He couldn't help hoping she'd understand.

After escaping from the enthusiastic Christopoulos family, and one dynamic Christopoulos male in particular, Annalise took some time to recover.

Although she wasn't sure there was enough time in the universe for her to recover from the emotions Niko Christopoulos set off inside her.

Right now, all she could say was that she liked being treated with such respect. He had been attuned to every word, every movement she made. The experience had been nerve-racking but very flattering, too.

But, then, from what she gathered from his family, all women thought the same about him. Smooth talking was not an asset in her book.

It was a lot to think about. She was sure she wouldn't be able to sleep tonight.

With the sun still up this close to the equator, the evening was still warm so she slipped on her shorts and T-shirt from earlier in the day and took a good long stroll around the deck's track, thinking of the love packed into those sincere family toasts. Afterwards, she ducked into one of the onboard kiosks to make herself a cup of hot decaf tea with the hope of swallowing down her envy for a life she could never be a part of.

Now Annalise breathed in the sea air as she took the stairs up to the adults-only top foredeck, carefully carrying her hot cup of tea to keep from spilling in the roughening seas. Although the wind was picking up, the temperature was still balmy.

Pinks and yellows colored the blue sky as the sun neared the horizon. At this time of year it would hang there for a good forty or so minutes before it plunged into the ocean. Watching the sunset was her favorite way to unwind and the tiny top foredeck was the perfect place to do it.

Most passengers found this little deck too tame. There was no pool, no wet T-shirt contests, no band and no elevator access. The three flights of stairs put off most people even if the lack of entertainment didn't.

So she was surprised to see someone sprawled out in her favorite deck chair as she rounded the platform at the top of the stairs.

And not just anyone. Niko.

She recognized him immediately, despite the dark sunglasses covering his eyes. His shirt was off as he reclined with his long legs crossed at the ankles, socks and loafers tucked underneath the deck chair.

That chest. Those pecs. If she didn't know better, she would think he'd been airbrushed. Dr. Christopoulos obviously didn't spend all his time in the operating room, lifting eyebrows and tightening chins. He had to spend a great deal of time at the gym as well.

This was not what she needed tonight. She turned to leave, then stopped herself.

No man was ever going to keep her from going where she wanted to go.

What was it about Niko Christopoulos that stirred up so much confusion inside her head?

When she could tear her focus away from his physique, she noticed his face. While his body looked peaceful in repose, his clenched jaw and compressed lips told a different story.

He looked like a man in internal pain.

Suddenly he half sat up, contracting those magnificent abs, and looked over the top of his sunglasses, straight at her. His features calmed, as if he pulled a mask over his emotions.

Had she made a noise? She didn't think so but she must have.

"Want to join me?" he asked.

As he made to stand up, she swallowed down all but the simplest of emotions and quickly said, "Please, keep your seat." The old-world manners made her feel special, even though she knew she wasn't. She pointed to the stairs behind her. "How's the leg?"

He shrugged. "The climb is worth it for the view."

The way he studied her over his sunglasses, she could almost imagine he was referring to her.

She could say no and probably would have if he had come on strong. There were plenty of empty deck chairs. She could say she just needed a few minutes of alone time. He would understand. Wasn't that what he was doing as well?

But he had invited her and she found herself moving in his direction before she could decline.

She picked out the deck chair next to his and

placed her tea next to the water bottle on the table between them. "Catching some rays?"

By the deepness of his tan, she knew it wouldn't be the first time. She couldn't imagine him in a tanning booth. Too artificial.

Hold on there, Annalise, she told herself. *This is a man who does artificial for a living.* Why was she assigning him qualities when she knew nothing about him?

He propped his chair up a few notches and reset his sunglasses on the top of his head.

The intensity in those tiger eyes of his mesmerized her so that she couldn't look away.

His voice was low, like a rumbling purr. "It's the wind. There's something about that unharnessed power, that cleansing force that attracts me." He rubbed his chin. "That sounded strange, didn't it?"

"Poetic." She held up her book, William Cullen Bryant. "I like poetry."

"Me, too." He gave her a grin and a wink.

He was flirting—with her!

There was a whole ship of beautiful women and he was coming on to her. But, then, there was no other woman around, which made her convenient, right?

She raised an eyebrow. "Really?"

Her reply was supposed to be a warning that

she knew his game and wasn't playing. Instead, it came out as a tease, as if she was taking up his challenge.

"Yup. Used to write it, too, under the guise of song lyrics."

"So you're a doctor and a musician? What's next? You're going to tell me you were a rock star in a boy band?"

"Only on my own block." He reset his sunglasses over his eyes. "Some friends and I had a garage band all through junior high and high school."

"Lead guitar?"

"Sometimes. Mostly drums. Some bass guitar. We switched around a lot."

"Did you sing?"

"Sometimes."

"I bet you had a motorcycle, too, didn't you?"

"An old Harley. I rebuilt it myself. And a black leather jacket—a hand-me-down from one of my brothers. I was really into the vintage rebel look." His self-deprecating laugh revealed two deep dimples.

"I'll just bet you were." With his dark looks she knew he'd pulled off the attitude perfectly. Surreptitiously, she glanced at his bare chest. He still did.

She winked at him. "From teenage heart throb to successful surgeon. Charmed life?"

She expected a flippant response. Instead, he thought about it for a moment then nodded slowly. "I've got a lot to be thankful for."

She wished she could see behind the shades. The moment hung in time, making an uneasiness spread through her. She shifted away.

While he didn't move a muscle, she felt him pulling back, too. Or was she only imagining it? What did she know of this man, except he was a compassionate doctor with the soul of a poet who, by the looks of things, managed his money well?

As she took a calming sip of tea, determined to treat this evening no differently than any other, he broke her concentration.

"Thanks for coming to my rescue this evening. They mean well, but they also think they know what's best for me."

"They're like those made-for-TV families. Are they always so nice? So genuine?"

"Nice? My family has good company manners. Genuine? Absolutely, even when it hurts. But I can call anyone, anytime, my sisters-in-law as well as my brothers, and they would drop everything to be there for me."

"And you'd do the same for them?"

He rubbed his hand over his face but failed to

disguise the tightening around his eyes and mouth. "I always have in the past."

"But not in the future?" Annalise immediately regretted her impulsive question. "I'm sorry. None of my business."

"It's not you. It's me." With a forced grin he shrugged away her apology as he spouted the classic meaningless cliché. "How about you? Judging by how quiet you were at dinner, I'm betting your family is a lot calmer than mine."

"No family. Just me." Her recent visit to her mother made her all too conscious of those bound together because of shared DNA. It wasn't a bond she willingly claimed.

"Here it comes." She pointed at the sun, resting on the horizon.

As if the big ball of flame had become too heavy to hold itself up, it plunged into the sea, taking with it all but a flat line of pinks and yellows and oranges to keep the sky separated from the water. Above that slim line of fading color, the night was dark and starry with nary a moonbeam in sight.

Around them, the deck's automatic twinkle lights began to glow.

Under the vastness of the night Annalise felt at peace with the world. She knew the feeling would be fleeting, with the responsibilities and decisions life would bring her, but she would enjoy that feeling while it lasted.

Next to her, Niko drew in a deep breath, held it then let it out again.

Having him near made her feel less alone than she'd felt in a very long time.

That surprised her. She had expected to feel like he was intruding on her special time. Instead, he made it even more special.

The serene minutes ticked away, giving her a false sense of permanence. When the squeaking and creaking of the pool boy's cart broke the silence, she wasn't surprised. Only sad that the moment was gone.

That's when she noticed the chill of the night air as it rushed over her bare legs. Reality. She'd been lucky to escape it for a few moments. To expect that kind of tranquility to last was unreasonable, wasn't it?

Reluctantly, Niko said a silent goodbye to the moment out of time he'd shared with Annalise.

He sat up and put on his shirt, socks and shoes. Normally, he would ask her to join him for a drink, trying to draw out the situation. But doing so tonight would only place expectations on a moment so rare it couldn't be coerced into lasting.

The good doctor lay with her head back and her eyes closed. The pose should be peaceful. Instead, he saw the tension that made the corners of her eyelids twitch and her involuntary jerk when the pool boy let the lid of his towel hamper slam shut.

He glanced at his watch. While he was certain his sister-in-law was taking care of Sophie as carefully as she took care of her own three children, he would check in on her.

Then maybe he would… He wasn't sure what he would do next. When was the last time he hadn't had a list of things in his head that he needed to do, all marked urgent?

As he climbed down the stairs, ignoring the burning in his thigh, he looked out at the dark, flat vastness of the sea. Three weeks.

Three long weeks with nowhere to be and nothing to do.

Why did he think of Annalise when he thought of how he would fill his time?

CHAPTER FOUR

DREAMS, WONDERFULLY WILDLY erotic dreams had made Annalise twist and turn all night. She knew they were normal, even healthy. While these were not her first, they had never been this vivid before.

Her lover had been faceless, nameless and frustrating since she awoke before he could take her where she wanted to go. If pressed, she was fairly certain she could name the source of those disturbing dreams. As disconcerting as they were, she was thrilled to be having them.

Annalise had put in many hours of therapy and self-assessment making sure she didn't stay a victim.

Those hours had not been in vain. She could fully appreciate sexual magnetism evoked by the sight of a good-looking male. A male like Niko Christopoulos, who was looking mighty fine this morning in his red baggy board shorts, tight sleeveless T-shirt and tennis shoes as he sat on a bench outside the medical suite, waiting for office hours to begin.

Irrationally, she wished she'd spent a little more time picking out her own clothing, which was silly. Her monochrome gray blouse and trousers were perfectly professional and practical, if not the cutting edge of fashion. But now they felt a little mousy.

Niko stared out at the ocean, lost in thought.

She cleared her throat to alert him she was there.

He blinked as he focused on her. "I didn't hear you come up."

"Is Sophie all right?"

"She's fine. Her blood sugar was low this morning when she woke up, but not too low. She barely protested when I checked it and gave her the breakfast insulin shot."

Last night's restless dreaming made her feel edgy when she asked, "Then why are you here?"

She winced when she heard herself. "Sorry. Restless night. Can I start again?"

Her problem was she knew how to rebuff male attention, but she didn't know what to do to encourage it. But maybe that was for the better. There were those ship's rules about fraternization to consider.

Still, a part of her, the wanton part left over from

last night no doubt, wondered what would be so wrong with a bit of flirtation. Just to satisfy her curiosity. With an experienced man like Niko it would be all in fun, right?

"No apology necessary. I know all about restless nights."

Much more civilly, she asked, "Do you have a medical problem?"

He rubbed his hand through his dark hair, spiking it out of order. "Actually, yes." He looked sheepish. "I've got something I need you to look at."

"Okay." She glanced at her watch. Her staff wouldn't be in for another half-hour. She usually preferred to have another staff member present when treating male patients. But it shouldn't matter in this case since they were both professionals. "Come on in."

As she unlocked the glass doors to the anteroom, Niko pointed to an envelope that had been slipped under the door. "A woman wearing a bartender's uniform, the one I met when I boarded, dropped that off for you."

"Thanks." Annalise pocketed the note. Concerned curiosity burned a hole in her pocket.

Once inside, Niko hitched himself up on the examination table and rolled up the right leg of his board shorts. A half-healed angry red cut at least five inches long sliced the side of his thigh. The stitches strained against the inflammation.

"What happened?"

He swallowed, then said, "A knife."

She narrowed her eyes. "I did my internship in the emergency departments of New Orleans's charity hospital system. I know a wickedly deliberate cut when I see it. This isn't from a steak knife or the slip of a pocket knife."

"I was caught in the middle of a knife fight over a water well in Haiti. So the infection could be tropical or it could be bacteria-related or—"

She put a thermometer in his mouth, making herself look away so she wouldn't stare at his firm, full lips or the rugged beard stubble on his cheeks. She didn't need any more stimulus to make her feel things—risky things—just because those tiger eyes were so mesmerizing.

And she didn't need to satisfy her curiosity by asking for details of his knife fight. The less she knew about him, the more easily she could convince herself they were just like two ships passing in the night.

When the thermometer beeped, he took it out himself, saving her from feeling his breath on her fingers.

"Ninety-nine and a half," he read.

"What have you been doing for your wound?"

"Topical ointment."

"That's all?"

He shrugged. "Antibiotics are in short supply there. I'm healthy, unlike the people I treat. I figured I could fight it off."

With that clue, Annalise couldn't stop herself from trying to put the pieces together. "You were treating patients when this happened?"

"I do a lot of medical relief work in developing countries." He looked down and away, as if he wasn't quite okay with himself for his charity work.

Annalise thought of the free clinics she visited and the donated supplies she delivered when assigned to various routes. She had been thinking hard about her volunteer service recently. "Any particular organization?"

"Doctors Without Borders."

"They really get into the trenches." She took a cotton swab from a sealed package. "I'm going to take a culture, but I don't want to wait for results so I'm going to give you a broad-spectrum oral antibiotic, too. Tomorrow, when I know what we're looking at, I can refine your treatment. Are you allergic to any medication?"

"Sulpha drugs."

"That limits us. How about penicillin-based drugs?"

"I'm good with those."

"I'll be right back." As Annalise left the exam room for the pharmacy closet, she took a deep breath. Success, brains, looks and heart. Being around so much perfection made her feel... She wasn't sure how she felt.

When she came back, he had rolled down the leg of his shorts and was standing in the open exam-room doorway. She handed him the bottle of antibiotic pills.

His fingers brushing against hers almost made her drop it.

"Two now, one each night and morning. Stay out of the water until we know what this is. Come back tomorrow afternoon for the test results."

"Thanks." He cast her a sideways look, half shy and half pleading. "By the way, my family doesn't know about the Doctors Without Borders gig. Please don't tell them."

"I'm very good at patient confidentiality. In fact, I swore an oath. They won't learn about it from me." Annalise stuck her hands in her pockets, feeling Brandy's note.

"I didn't mean any insult. It's just that..." He

stopped and held the pills up between them. "Thanks again."

Secrets. Why on earth would he want something that noble to remain a secret from his family? It wasn't her business, though, was it?

Still, it bothered her. Secrets made her think of lies. Was he lying to her?

Annalise hated secrets more than anything else on earth. How many times had her mother whispered "Don't tell…" as she was juggling men in her life? Then there had been the man who'd whispered "Don't tell" as he'd crept into her bedroom when her mother hadn't been home.

Annalise pulled out the note and read it.

"Doc, I need an appointment, but I'm working during your office hours and I don't want my shift manager to know. Could I come in after hours? Drop by the bar and let me know, okay? Brandy."

Annalise sighed. No doubt her tattoo had become infected.

The bell tinkled, signaling patients in the lobby. She quickly filled out a chart for Niko—Dr. Christopoulos—as she readied herself for the next patient.

As Caribbean music played softly from the overhead speakers, Annalise reminded herself that her life was totally what she'd made it and so far she hadn't done half-bad. Just keep it simple, she reminded herself.

And simple didn't include Niko Christopoulos.

Simple obsession. That's the only reason that could explain why, on a ship carrying several thousand people, Niko caught her attention as she took her afternoon break on deck.

She'd thought about him all day. His playboy image. His love for his family. His compassion with Sophie. His work with Doctors Without Borders. There was nothing simple about Niko and no simple explanation for why her feet were now carrying her straight towards him.

On the first full afternoon afloat, the ship was alive with activity and the Christopoulos family was doing its fair share to add to the frivolity.

Niko stood contemplating the rock wall. His older nephews had their harnesses strapped on and were waiting. Niko was not one to turn down a challenge.

He felt her before he heard her. Even though they barely knew each other, he knew the warmth by his side was uniquely Annalise.

"It's going to be difficult to keep that wound a

secret if you break open the stitches halfway up," she murmured, for his ears only.

"The voice of reason. Where have you been all my life?" He waved is nephews on. "I've found something better to do," he called to them.

Marcus looked pointedly at Annalise then jostled his brother and grinned.

Annalise arched an eyebrow. "Are you being presumptuous by meaning me?"

"Let's not call it presumptuous. Let's call it hopeful." He gave her his best puppy-dog eyes. "Want to watch for dolphins off the starboard bow with me?"

When she hesitated, he appealed to her medical side. "You'll be keeping me from doing something stupidly injurious to my health."

"Are you sure it's not too late? I think you've already fallen on your head one time too many since you've chosen me to flirt with."

"Flirt?" He grabbed at his chest. "You've wounded me. I would never toy with your affections." Yet wasn't that exactly what he was doing?

No. No, it wasn't.

Annalise lived on a cruise ship. No permanence there. She would know the score. There was no serious romance involved, just a casual attraction that would end at their final destination.

"Of course you're not flirting with me. Why would you when there are plenty of toys in this floating toy box?" Although she smiled when she said it, Niko thought he saw a bleakness cross her eyes or maybe it was only a cloud crossing the sun.

Before he could decide, she blinked and the fleeting look was gone.

"Ready? The dolphins won't wait." She led the way, weaving in and out of the passengers on deck.

"Thank you for rescuing me from myself. When the twins dared me, I didn't have it in me not to race them up. If you hadn't come along when you did, I would be halfway up the rock wall by now and my thigh wound wouldn't have appreciated my bravado."

"You have a hard time turning down a challenge?"

"Challenges are just another word for thrills for me. And you?"

She stopped at the railing and looked out on the sun-sparkled sea. "Challenges bring out the stubbornness in me."

"I've always thought stubbornness was a very good trait to have."

"Others would disagree." Very subtly, Annalise shifted away from him. Niko doubted she even realized she'd done it.

"Those *others* don't understand how much determination it takes to get through medical school."

"Determination. Scholarships. Student loans. Lots and lots of caffeine." She rubbed her arms. "And, occasionally, the kindness of the few others who do understand."

"Or who support you even when they don't understand." Niko thought of all the sandwiches his brothers had brought him as he'd studied past midnight. Of all the twenty-dollar bills his grandmother had slipped into his pockets after she'd laundered his clothes.

"Like your family?"

"Like my family." The family who wouldn't be at all happy with his new career path. "So where'd you go to medical school?"

"Tulane. I went there for both medical school and undergraduate pre-med."

Niko raise his eyebrows at the mention of the exclusive private college in uptown New Orleans's Audubon Park district. "Wow! I'm impressed.

"Did you grow up in New Orleans? The Crescent City has a thousand accents, but I think I hear a hint of a traditional New Orleans drawl, don't I?"

Her mouth tightened at the corners before she answered, "Yes, I did."

"What part?"

"It doesn't matter. Hurricane Katrina wiped it out." She shuddered, as if she was shaking off memories, before she forced out a smile. "Your turn. Where did you go to medical school?"

"The local state university."

"Ah, home of the Tigers. Did you play sports?"

"No." He grinned. "Even though that's their reputation, not everyone does—but I did drink a lot of beer. And you?"

"Beer or sports?" She smiled back, her face lighting up like sunbeams shone on it.

Niko soaked in her glow. "Either."

"Neither. I was on academic scholarship. No money for beer and no time for sports. I held a couple of part-time jobs, so that kept me busy when I wasn't studying. I was rather boring back then, I'm afraid."

"You, boring? Not possible. More like admirable to make it through Tulane's medical school while working, too." Niko once again realized how much his family had given him. "I worked at the restaurant on occasion and did a few odd jobs here and there, especially during the summers. But generally I had it pretty good."

"One of my jobs was as a dog washer for a local vet. I really liked working with the dogs. It wasn't a bad job—just messy and smelly."

"Did you ever think of switching to veterinary medicine?"

"Nope. I'm allergic to cats."

"Not many cats on a cruise ship."

"Not a single one on this ship."

"There's quite a bit of difference between working in an inner city E.R. and working on a cruise ship, I'd imagine."

Giving him a thoughtful look somewhere between sunshine and shadow, Annalise answered, "I like a bit of challenge, too. New places, new people, a diversity of problems to be solved. The E.R. took care of two out of three, but a cruise ship takes care of all three."

"Itchy feet. I understand all too well that the thrill of adventure gets your adrenaline rushing."

"As far as adrenaline rushes go, I can't say a cruise ship compares to being airlifted into a developing country, but we try." She grinned, showing off a dimple as she shaded her eyes and scanned the water for dolphins. How could she be so unaware of her beauty?

"That's what the brochure said."

"So what thrilling adventures have you had this morning?"

He had spent considerable time watching a very enjoyable wet T-shirt contest with the twins but he decided to tell her about the starfish demonstration he'd attended with his younger nieces and nephews instead.

"I had no idea starfish could regenerate body parts."

"Fascinating." She gave him a wry look. "Anything else?"

"Lunch with the family. Dining with them is always a major event, for us and for everyone around us. My brothers had to have a taste of every kind of bread in the basket to analyze taste and texture. The little ones spilled one glass of milk and one glass of orange juice in quick succession. And Sophie decided she wasn't hungry. Making her eat to balance out her morning insulin shot was a real challenge."

"How did you do it?"

"Yiayia gave her the evil eye. It always works." He'd had a long talk with Yiayia last night about Sophie's juvenile diabetes. While she didn't understand everything, she finally did understand the importance of working with Sophie's caregivers instead of against them.

"Your grandmother is very special to you, isn't she?"

"She raised me. I owe her and my brothers everything." He rubbed his hand across his eyes. He didn't like to talk about it. So why was he about to tell Annalise?

"My parents died when I was young. The three of us were in a car wreck." He left out the details about being stranded in the car with them for hours while the rescue workers had tried to save them all.

"It's why I hate goodbyes." As if compelled, he found himself confessing, "Before they died, they both told me they loved me. I didn't understand. I had the chance but didn't take it. I thought, if I didn't say goodbye to them, they would live."

"How old were you?"

"Eight." He stared out at the vast ocean all around. "My brothers were sixteen, fourteen and thirteen then. They buried their grief, trying to help me recover from mine. They had to grow up so fast for me. Along with Yiayia, they've been taking care of me ever since. They've never once complained about their lot in life."

"Your family finds strength in each other. I saw that last night at the dinner table."

He gave her a wry look. "And then there's me."

"You're different?"

He nodded confirmation. "I'm different."

"How?"

"I love my family but I often feel trapped, smothered. Uncomfortable in my own skin." He'd never said any of this out loud. Not even to himself in the dark of night. Why now? Why Annalise?

Was it because they were complete strangers and would never see each other after this trip ended?

He'd had so much on his mind and in his heart for so many years. Recently, since he'd started to consider selling his portion of the practice, the pressure had been building more and more until he thought he would come apart at the seams.

"They've sacrificed so much to give me a comfortable lifestyle they'd never even dream of having themselves."

And he had been determined to succeed for them. To give back to them. To show his appreciation by being all they wanted him to be.

"They're very proud of you. Even when your brothers tease you, they do it with pride in their voices. And your grandmother told me at least a dozen times how you have big-time celebrities for clientele." Realization dawned. "You're afraid of disappointing them. How could you? You've become everything they sacrificed for. You've fulfilled their expectations. They get to be in the limelight through you, and I think they're perfectly happy that way."

"But that's not me." He struggled with being that man they imagined him to be. The one who strutted onto talk shows to talk about celebrity makeovers or who attended black-tie affairs with a model on his arm. The whole time he sipped champagne and waved away expensive hors d'oeuvres he thought of those who didn't have the basics of clean water to drink or food to eat.

"The sparkle in Yiayia's eyes when she brags about my photos on the society pages of the newspapers can't erase the bleakness in the eyes of the mothers whose children suffer from cleft palates. Doctors Without Borders. That's where I belong. No fanfare. No glory."

No family. That part was too painful to say aloud. Giving up the happiness his brothers had found in the arms of the women they loved had been a decision he'd willfully made but he still couldn't stop wishing he could have it all.

But his wandering ways didn't make for permanent relationships. A woman needed things. A house full of knick-knacks and baubles, a steady group of friends, children. Permanence. All the things he couldn't promise her.

"You've chosen a tough path."

He nodded. "But I need it. I'm never more alive than when I'm cheating death. I need the deeply satisfying buzz of seeing blank eyes start to sparkle, of seeing hope come alive in environments and conditions that make living from day to day a challenge."

His world was not one where he would voluntarily raise a family.

"I can see that in you. I hear the passion in your voice." Her own voice quavered, as if she was hesitant to offer that much up to him. "Why medicine? There are a lot of professions you could have chosen."

He shrugged. "Most of my memories of the wreck are fuzzy, just a lot of hazy pain, emotional more than physical, I think. I broke my jaw but I don't remember it hurting all that much right then. They sent a helicopter. There were flashing lights and rain and loud voices over the police cars' speaker systems.

"But through it all there was this doctor who crawled into the wreckage and held my hand while they cut my parents out. He promised me he wouldn't let go until I was free and he talked to me the whole time. He was calm and sure when my world was in total chaos. He was my hero. I wanted to be just like him."

Niko wiped at his eyes with the back of his hand. "I've never told anyone—no one's ever asked before."

The silence stretched awkwardly as he looked

out at the ocean, feeling the loss of his parents, remembering the hours he'd waited alone for rescue. Knowing how he often felt alone even now, despite the love of his family throughout the years.

Annalise startled him when she covered his hand with her own. She didn't say anything. She didn't even look at him. She just stared out at the ocean, too. But with her hand on his, he didn't feel so alone.

A movement against the waves caught his attention.

"There they are." With his free hand, he pointed at the magnificent mammals playing in the waves.

Annalise shielded her eyes with her free hand. "Four of them."

Two small dolphins played among the larger ones. "A family."

"Their families are called pods. It's a matriarchal structure." Annalise smiled as one of the dolphins broke away from the group and started twisting itself above the waves.

"I'm very familiar with that structure." Niko watched the baby dolphin jump and spin. "There's always one that's got to be different."

She squeezed his hand. "That's not a bad thing."

When the dolphin had done a half dozen jumping

twists, he swam back to his pod, where the other dolphins bumped noses in greeting.

The wind blew Annalise's hair into her face. He reached up to brush it back, but something in her eyes made him hesitate and he wrapped his fingers around the railing instead.

She released his hand to push the errant strands away herself. "That must be the dolphin version of a family hug."

She had given him the perfect opening. "How about your family?"

Her lips took on a wry twist. "In some animal species, the mothers eat their young."

She brushed off the hair on her check as she lost the brightness in her face. Her eyes looked bruised and sad.

Niko would do anything to wipe that sadness from her soul. But he had a feeling that would take a lot of time and patience and he only had a few weeks.

Then her eyes went blank, making him doubt what he'd seen just seconds before. She took a quick step away from him, glancing at her watch and clearly backing away from the intimacy they had shared. "I've got to go—"

"Back to work?" He said it for her, saving her the indignity of uttering the time-worn excuse.

When he'd picked up Sophie's new insulin vial after lunch, he'd already been told the doctor had taken the early shift and was off for the rest of the day.

Obviously, he had mistaken the good doctor's compassion for something more. He wasn't sure what he'd wanted that "more" to be.

Even though she hadn't moved a muscle, he could feel her pulling away. "Niko, this is supposed to be your vacation, a time for fun and recharging."

"Not a soul-searching expedition." He felt rebuffed and more than a little embarrassed. Spilling his guts wasn't something he usually did with a woman—especially a woman he just met and had no intention of getting to know beyond these three weeks out of time. Just because he felt a pull toward her didn't mean she felt it too, or that she had to respond even if she did.

Her forced smile was so very different from her natural one. "Make sure your fun doesn't stress your wound."

This *was* a time for fun, not a time for deep reflection—most particularly about a woman he'd just met and would never see again after his fun was over.

His perspective restored, he nodded. "Sure thing, Doc. I've used work as an excuse myself a few times. I didn't mean to keep you from your patients. And I've got umbrella drinks to try. Maybe I'll catch you later."

Walking away was the right thing to do. Why was it so hard?

Because he never backed down from a challenge, right? That had to be the reason. But maybe this time he should. Life was too short...

From now on, when a woman flirted with him on deck, he would flirt back, buy her a drink, enjoy her company with the understanding they were both stealing a moment in a fantasy world that would come to an end when the cruise ended. He would take advantage of this time that had nothing to do with his reality and enjoy himself.

Then, during those long nights under mosquito nets, he would pull out the memories, have a smile, and find the energy to get back to work in the morning.

As he headed toward the big-haired brunette, the one that was supposed to be his type, he could feel Annalise's eyes on him, watching him.

When he looked back to be sure, he kept his sunglasses securely in place as he flashed her a cocky grin, deliberately hiding his reaction to a woman who moved him like no woman ever had before.

"Is this seat taken?" he asked the brunette.

She had more than enough appreciation in her eyes to soothe his ego, right?

She greeted him with a sweep of her hand to indicate the empty chair. "I've been saving it for you."

Niko let out a deep breath. This woman knew the game. Now to have some fun.

"What are we drinking?"

"I recommend the rum punch." She welcomed him with a raised glass and a gleamingly bright smile. "I'm Helena. Your grandmother said we should meet." Her Greek accent verified her heritage.

She was everything he should want in a woman, especially one who was only temporary.

If only he could be less aware of the reluctant little honey-haired blonde walking away from him and more interested in the eager brunette right in front of him, he would make a lot of people very happy—including himself.

The waiter brought over a tray holding huge glasses filled with enough fruit to host a luau. The paper umbrellas wilted against the condensation on the glasses. Definitely not his kind of drink. He thought about asking for a beer instead, but that would mean he'd have to stay around and wait for it to be delivered and he wasn't sure he wanted to stay that long.

"Your grandmother tells me you're single?"

Niko nodded confirmation.

"I'm divorced." Helen took a deep sip from the new glass and shrugged, as if it didn't matter, but her eyes said it really did.

Niko sipped his too-sweet drink and tried to look sympathetic. He'd heard so many domestic tales of woe that all he got from the conversation was validation that he was not made for marriage. "Sorry it didn't work out."

"Me, too. My ex-husband was a Texas oil tycoon. Sadly, after I turned thirty-five, he became more interested in drilling holes than in me."

"So you're going back home?"

"To visit. Maybe to stay. I'm not sure yet." The way she said it, she sounded like staying wasn't her first choice.

"We're on a family vacation. My grandmother is going to show us her homeland."

"I know. I met your Yiayia. She tells me you're a very successful cosmetic surgeon who's been on television and works on celebrities."

"Maxiofacial surgeon." He gave her his best smoldering look. Somehow, it felt more manipulative than usual. "I can see you don't need my services."

But Helen knew the game. She batted her eyelashes at him. "And here I was thinking you'd be good at popping a champagne bottle cork. Tonight? My balcony?"

It was the kind of invitation he'd hoped to get when he'd boarded the ship. But now all he could think of was sharing a sunset beer or cup of tea with Annalise on the foredeck again.

When he didn't answer right away, she gave him a hard look. "Not interested?"

"As much as I'd like to, I'm here for my family this trip."

"Sure." Her smile was bitter. "I guess my ex was right."

Yes, she knew the game well, fishing for a compliment to negate the ex-husband's harshness. He had a list of phrases he used in situations like this. Why couldn't he think of an appropriate one?

"I hope your homecoming is everything you expect it to be."

He left the drink on a tray, excused himself and determined to be anywhere she wasn't.

It wasn't Helena, who appeared to be perfectly perfect. It was him. He was so tired of playing the game.

Annalise didn't even know there was a game, much less how to play.

Niko suddenly felt very good about his decision. Helena was the kind of trouble he didn't need.

But, then, all women came with a certain amount of trouble, didn't they?

Why did Annalise seem worth it when all the other women didn't?

While he didn't believe in love at first sight, he now had first-hand knowledge that obsession at first sight was a very real phenomenon.

CHAPTER FIVE

ANNALISE DUCKED INTO an elevator and hit the button to close the door just as she began to shake. The intensity of emotion Niko had shared with her had caught her off balance. She'd wanted to reach out and hold him tight, to take away the pain in his heart, to make him all better.

But all she'd managed to do had been to touch his hand then make a hasty retreat before the conversation turned deep again. Sharing secrets about her own family would have been more than she could have handled.

As always, she hid behind her work, just like Niko had accused her of doing. It was all she had.

Annalise spent the rest of her afternoon off in the office, helping her new physician's assistant get settled into the ship's routine.

The work was familiar. Safe. Unexciting.

Unlike the way she felt around Niko.

As she worked, she couldn't keep herself from

thinking of all she was missing, keeping herself apart and safe. And unexciting.

In fact, she would have to describe her life as downright boring.

For the first time ever, she craved a thrill down her spine, the kind of thrill she got when Niko was near. She wasn't sure what she should do about it but she was certain her lack of ability to handle her emotions had come across to Niko as disinterest.

That buxom brunette certainly had no problem projecting her interest, had she?

As she and her P.A. documented inventory and filed their charts, she was glad that the P.A was either in too chatty a frame of mind or was discreet enough to pretend not to notice her mercurial mood.

With only a fraction of her attention Annalise listened to her talk about leaving her fiancé at the altar.

"I figure I'll do this for a while, maybe a year. Then, when all the fuss dies down, I'll go back home."

While some did it for the adventure, the P.A. was one of many who had chosen to work on a cruise ship to run from bad history. She and Annalise had that in common.

Annalise responded, to be nice. "Better to break up before the marriage than after, right?"

She didn't add that it was even better to break up before the preacher and congregation were seated, waiting for the bride to walk down the aisle, like her new P.A. had done. That was an opinion better kept to herself.

But her P.A. seemed to be competent in her work. The way she managed her love life was none of Annalise's concern.

Then, again, with Annalise's lack of experience she really didn't have much basis on which to judge these matters of the heart.

Was Niko a love-'em-and-leave-'em kind of guy? From what his family said about him, she'd just bet he was.

"So what's your story, Doc? The contract office said you'd been sailing longer than any other doctor they had signed up."

This was not a conversation Annalise wanted to have. Her dread must have shown on her face because the P.A quickly followed up with, "They said it in a good way. That you were the best to learn from. But you've been doing this for a while, haven't you?"

"Yes, I have." The normal explanation would be that she was still running away, and maybe that was correct, but she had no intention of discussing her personal hang-ups with anyone other than her therapist. Hopefully, her tone would discourage any further conversation along this line.

Her contract was up when they made port in Malaga, Spain. She had an option to extend her tour of service to cover the extra week the ship would be looping through the Greek isles, but was thinking hard about whether she wanted to sign another contract at the end of this trip.

Regardless of her reasons, putting down roots in her home town of New Orleans, or in any one particular place in the world, held no appeal for her.

She'd been thinking about Niko and his charity work ever since she'd examined his knife wound. Maybe she'd find a private moment to ask more. It would be a legitimate reason to see him again instead of a trumped-up excuse.

And just maybe he wouldn't reject her like she had rejected him.

Tonight? On the foredeck? Annalise didn't believe in happenstance, but maybe this once she could allow herself to believe that if it was meant to be, it would happen.

Niko and his brothers and sisters-in-law had been hitting the "golf balls" made of fish food off the back of the ship for over an hour now. Watching the fish school to eat the "golf balls" made Yiayia and the children smile.

He teed up the fish-food golf ball and concentrated on swinging the club. Or at least he tried to concentrate on his swing. Even though he'd vowed to put Annalise from his mind, he hadn't been able to do it.

As he shanked his shot, he realized what had been nagging at him. That blank expression on her face when he'd asked about her family. He'd seen that look before—from victims trying to cope.

The thought of anyone anywhere hurting Annalise sent a burst of rage through him.

He teed up another fish ball and swung, hooking this one but sending it further than any of his previous hits.

Stephen put his hand on Niko's shoulder.

"Don't frown, little brother. I'll show you how it's done."

Marcus teed up his own ball. "Because we've been taking lessons. Right, Dad?"

Hearing his brothers' hearty laughter emphasized how much he had in his family.

And how much Annalise didn't have. As she had comforted him, he wanted to comfort her, give her a shoulder, let her know…

Know what? That he would always be there for her?

He couldn't promise that to any woman. The places he went, the things he did made commitment to a woman impossible. He was actually grateful to his ex for showing him the futility of trying to have it all.

"It's only fair that I pass on what I've learned." Stephen looked Niko in the eye, more serious than usual. "After all, thanks to my baby brother buying into the restaurant, we've been able to hire another manager so I can take the occasional afternoon off now and spend more time with my sons. I can never thank you enough for that, little brother."

"After all you've done for me, it's me that is in your debt." Niko grinned. "But I bet you a beer I can hit this next one farther than you can."

"I'll take a side bet on Niko." Phoebe grinned at them both. "Don't you know that doctors know how to play golf? It comes with the diploma. I'll bet you play at all those fancy resorts you keep running off to."

"I'll take that side bet, Mom. I'll bet Uncle Niko doesn't play a lot of golf when he's out of town." Marcus gave Niko a strong stare. "Ask his ex-fiancée. He's not like most doctors."

What had his ex told Marcus now? Had she broken her promise to keep his charity work secret?

Phoebe patted Niko on the shoulder in case he needed comforting. "It will take a strong woman to keep our Niko's attention.

Annalise. Why did he think of her when he thought of a strong woman? He didn't even know her.

Could she live on canned beans and peaches for ten days straight because the supply truck had been hijacked? Could she sleep on the ground under a mosquito net because the wind was too strong to pitch a tent with a hurricane blowing in off the coast? Could she complete surgery as rebel gunfire threatened to overrun an encampment?

That's the kind of superwoman that would fit into Niko's life.

He had to grin as he thought of Annalise draping the superhero cape around Sophie's shoulders. Going from cruise ship to jungle boat would take a superhuman leap—a leap he could never expect anyone to take on his behalf.

He squared up to hit the last fish-food golf ball into the ocean.

Sophie jumped up and down and pointed at the splash he'd made. "Hey, look how far Uncle Niko hit it! He just beat everybody."

As one, his family turned and applauded him. That's what the Christopoulos family did when you met expectations. They cheered you on.

He'd never let them down yet. What would happen when he did?

As Annalise was unlocking the etched-glass doors leading into the medical suite to accommodate Brandy's off-hours request, the bartender rushed up to her.

"Doc, you're here." Her face showed panic and her voice was on the edge of hysteria.

Annalise pushed open the doors. "Come in. What's wrong?"

"How could I forget? And now…" Brandy bit her knuckle. "Now I think I'm pregnant."

"You were fine when we boarded. What happened between then and now?" Annalise tried to put the pieces together. "Did you have unprotected sex recently?"

"No. Yes. Well, not within the last day or so, anyway." Brandy wrapped her arms around herself. "I can't have a baby, not the way I live. What will I do with it?"

A sympathetic knot formed in Annalise's stomach. She squelched it down, intellectually keeping her own personal experience safely dissociated from her patient's. Emotionally keeping her distance was more of a challenge. But overlying Brandy's circumstances with her own personal trauma wouldn't be good for either of them.

"Let's talk about it back here." Annalise ushered her back to an examination room, seated her in a chair and took out her clipboard with a fresh chart. "How many days has it been since your last period?"

"I don't know. I don't keep up with it, really, since I use the kind of birth control that keeps you from having one very often. But I've been feeling a little tired and my roommate says she's noticed I've put on weight." Brandy patted her gently rounded stomach. "I feel puffy and my breasts are really tender. Once my roommate pointed it out to me, it was obvious. All the signs are there."

"What type of birth control do you use?"

"The patch." Brandy looked down at the floor. "But I think I forgot to change it."

She looked up, desperation in her eyes. "What am I going to do, Doc?"

Annalise hated that question. She was duty-bound to discuss options, but she knew all too well all the choices would have life-changing consequences.

Annalise stared down at the blank form, using

her analytical training to compose herself. "The first thing to do is take a pregnancy test. Test your urine first thing in the morning when the hormones will be more concentrated. If the test comes back positive, we'll do an ultrasound to try to determine how long you've been pregnant."

She took a pregnancy testing kit from an overhead cabinet and handed it to Brandy. Brandy hugged it to her chest like a lifeline.

"And then?"

"And then I'll give you some information and you can make some decisions." Three weeks. They would be out at sea for three weeks. So many things hung in the balance.

The wild look in Brandy's eyes worried Annalise. Even though she wasn't keen on personal touching, she felt compelled to cover the bartender's hand with her own.

"A strong support system will help you through this, Brandy. Your parents? Siblings? I can set you up with a ship-to-shore line and you can give them a call."

Brandy shook her head. "We're not that kind of a family."

"We can't all be that lucky, can we?" Annalise thought of the Christopoulos clan. Even though she'd only seen them in action a few times, she knew they would rally round one of their own, giving comfort and security.

Hesitantly, she asked, "What about the father? Would he be supportive of you?" When she thought about support, why did Niko come to mind? She'd barely met the man. Why did she cast him in the role of protector?

Brandy looked up at the ceiling, hugging herself tight and rocking back and forth. "I'm still thinking about that one."

"Promise me you won't do anything rash or stupid."

Brandy flushed as if Annalise had caught her in the act. She stood, hugging the pregnancy test box to her chest. "I promise, Doc."

"See you in the morning, then. Have me paged if you need me before that."

With a nod Brandy was gone, leaving Annalise with a quiet, sterile room and too many painful memories.

Needing alone time, Niko rushed through supper with his family. He loved them, each and every one of them. But they were so—so *there* all the time, like a litter of puppies, rolling over each other, playfully nipping at each other, never letting a littermate out of sight.

He settled into the lounge chair he'd claimed the night before. Board shorts, barefoot, beer in hand, now he could breathe deeply. He toasted the ocean, thinking of all the toasts his family had just saluted each other with. Too many of those toasts had to do with him finding the perfect woman, settling down, starting a family. They had drunk *to his future happiness!*

And to theirs, he'd toasted back, his lemon-twisted water standing out in stark contrast against his brothers' rich merlots.

He'd had enough wine the night before to last him a while. Unlike his family's preference, wine wasn't his favorite. Just like attending tomorrow's tour of the cruise-ship kitchens was a field trip he'd opted to skip.

Only a few days out and he was already prowling the decks. This low level of activity wasn't good for him, tying him up in knots instead of letting him relax.

That sixth sense that had kept him safe innumerable times in the past told him she was approaching. Annalise.

"Is this seat taken?" Something in her eyes looked vulnerable, hopeful. Anxious. "Can I sit here?"

Something in his heart couldn't say no.

Waves of emotion surged through him. What he was feeling for her was more than the foam that short-term flings were made from.

He could so easily drown in the deep blue depths of her eyes.

The smart thing to do would be to explain his need for privacy. It was a valid answer. But he found himself saying, "I was saving it for you."

And he found himself realizing that's exactly what he had been doing.

She looked at him, looked hard enough he felt compelled to push his sunglasses to the top of his head.

"Hard day?" she asked.

He flashed her his celebrity smile. "I'm on a cruise ship. Is there such a thing as a hard day?"

Her eyes said it all. She was disappointed in him for skirting her question. He wanted to redeem himself very badly.

"I'm not used to doing nothing. It feels so…trivial."

"Tell me about Doctors Without Borders." Gracefully, she sank into the lounge chair without spilling a drop from the cup of hot tea she balanced on her saucer.

"What do you want to know?"

She leaned forward, as if she wanted to catch

each word before the wind tore it away. As if what he said held great import. As if *he* were of great import. "Where was your first mission?"

So he told her about the trauma care facility in Northern Afghanistan and about how hours of operating made a person numb to the dangers around them.

"The real danger is becoming numb to the people around you. But there was always someone—a father or sister or friend—who reminded you that your patients weren't just bodies that needed medical attention but loved ones who needed medical care."

He couldn't imagine trying to explain this to anyone else, but with Annalise he could see the understanding in her eyes.

Her hands clenched and unclenched around her tea cup. "I was in my first semester of rotation in the E.R. during Hurricane Katrina. In my mind, everything runs together after those first forty-eight hours."

She took a sip of her tea. "What was your first assignment?"

"The tsunami."

"Tell me about it."

He talked for hours, longer than he'd ever spoken about his work before. And she listened, asked questions, nodded sympathetically and laughed at the humorous stories the human psyche needed to break up the horror of it all.

He fell asleep sometime during the evening and when he awoke with the stars gleaming overhead she'd covered him with a blanket against the night air.

CHAPTER SIX

SADLY, ANNALISE HAD had no erotic dreams during the night but she had fallen asleep with Niko on her mind and woken up thinking of him, too. She certainly wouldn't call her night restful. Who would have guessed such a heroic heart beat beneath that pretty boy rebel exterior?

Annalise went down to the medical suite as soon as the early morning yoga class on deck was dismissed. Brandy was usually in that class, but today she was a no-show.

It must have been one of the longest nights of Brandy's life. Annalise's heart went out to her.

When Annalise had realized she was pregnant she'd been almost as frightened as when—

The bell signaling patients arriving kept Annalise from going down a path she'd rather never travel again.

Like it always did, helping others took her mind off her own concerns. Annalise had a steady stream of patients with sunburn from strong tropical rays that took them by surprise and acid reflux from overindulging, both typical complaints at this point in a cruise.

Halfway through her shift one of her receptionists delivered a note, sealed and addressed to her, that had been left at the front counter.

Annalise opened the note. "Not pregnant. Relieved, but kind of sad, too. Am putting on a new patch this morning. Brandy."

Simply apply a patch and go on with life. It was an uncomplicated way to handle a shipboard romance.

So why did Niko and complications pop into her head just as she was confirming her desire for the simple life?

After an hour of wandering around the ship, trying to accidently bump into Niko, Annalise finally spotted him wandering aimlessly around the main pool area. Instead of rushing up to him, she stayed back and observed him for a while. What was it about him that compelled her to watch him? Was it his natural good looks? Or the way his black wavy hair fell onto his forehead in that perfectly casual way? Or the way his T-shirt stretched across his muscled shoulders? Or was it the way he moved, strong and lethal like the tiger she saw in his eyes?

Or maybe it was the way those eyes lit up when he talked about fixing a cleft palate on a little girl and seeing her smile years later when he was re-assigned to the same area.

She tried not to notice as she stood next to a high table near her favorite kiosk and dunked her tea bag into her cup of hot water. But as she stirred sugar into her afternoon tea her attention kept returning to him.

He sat at the bar for a while, ordered a beer, then moved toward the lounge chairs, but decided to look over the railing instead.

She had expected to see a playboy on the prowl. Instead, she saw a man alone who didn't know what to do with himself. She had the strongest urge to offer suggestions—suggestions that included her company.

As if he could hear her thoughts, he turned from the rail, scanned the crowd and found her.

"Annalise."

Through the noisy crowd she couldn't hear him, but she could read his lips. In the past, if a passenger wanted to get friendly, she would wave him off and move on, but she couldn't put Niko into the same class as just another passenger. So when he walked towards her, she stood still and waited for him.

"Hey, you." He pushed his sunglasses to the top of his head and gave her a movie-star grin that almost made her swoon. She barely stopped herself from looking around to see who he was really talking to.

If she had been diagnosing herself, she would have had to say her palpitations were the results a developmentally delayed teenage crush.

"Hey you back," she managed to say, pleased that she didn't sound at all bedazzled. "Just hanging out at the pool?"

"I threw a penny in the wishing well a moment ago. That thing really works."

"You got your wish already?"

"Yup. I wished a beautiful woman would come up and talk to me and here you are."

Self-consciously Annalise pulled down the hem of her new orange tank top, which she'd layered over her new bright yellow one, and wiggled her newly painted toenails exposed by her new beaded leather sandals. It was silly to feel self-conscious amongst all the string bikinis on deck.

"Thanks." She didn't need the glance in the glass doors that separated the cruise ship's interior from its exterior to remind her that she was showing a lot more skin than she normally did. She usually only wore tank tops under shirts or thin blouses.

But something—or, if she was honest, someone—had inspired a shopping spree.

She might not be as sophisticated as that Greek woman but, still, she'd not done too badly, if she did say so herself.

He kept staring into her eyes. She realized she'd been staring back and blinked.

"So, what did you do today?"

He took a deep sip from the drink he carried. "I played bingo with Yiayia for a while this morning. I won a T-shirt and she won a key chain. Then I went to the kids Underwater Explorers' activity, where we learned about submarines. The twins are on the water slides, but my doctor grounded me from that. And the rest of the family is attending a pastry-making school. Can you believe it? They all cook for a living, but they go on vacation and now they're cooking again."

"I guess they love what they do."

"I guess so." He shrugged, giving her a crooked grin. "If the ship offered a seminar on reconstructing sinus cavities, I'd probably be in the front row."

The wry expression on his face made her laugh. "You should drop off that suggestion at Guest Services. They're always open to new ideas."

The smile he flashed reached all the way to his

eyes. She hadn't realized how brilliant those eyes could be. They took her breath away.

But the sparkle didn't last long. "I was just wondering what to do next. Any suggestions?"

She consulted the flyer listing the day's activities, which she'd picked up after her pedicure, and picked the first thing on the list. "I'm going to the gourmet coffee tasting. Want to come?"

He leaned in close to read the paper she held. "I'll go anywhere with you."

The way he said it, so low and intimate, sent shivers through her. Practically, she wondered how many women he'd practiced on before he'd got that timbre just right.

He gave her a quizzical look. "What?"

"Just you and your pick-up lines."

"You don't like them?"

"I didn't say that." She looked up into those glistening eyes. "They just aren't necessary. I like you fine without all the swagger."

He pulled his sunglasses over his eyes. "But without the swagger, what do I have?"

Apparently, she'd hit a sore spot. This man-woman interplay wasn't her forte. She started walking toward the coffee shop.

The silence between them felt awkward and needed filling.

Annalise said what was on her mind, hoping her honesty didn't get her into worse trouble. "If you're fishing for a compliment, I can give you several. You're talented, according to your prestigious client list. You're generous. Brave. Good with children. Should I go on?"

She didn't know someone so deeply tanned—or so cocky—could blush as deeply as he did.

"If you keep it up, I'll have to hire you as my publicist."

"Do you have one?"

He gave her a sideways glance. "Uh—no. I'm a serious working doctor, no matter what you've heard from my grandmother."

"She's very proud of you."

"She's proud of all of us."

"I didn't hear her bragging about your brothers at supper the other night."

"Magazine covers and TV interviews impress her." He stopped outside the café's entrance. "It was all to build the practice. Thankfully, it worked. I keep telling my brothers they need to do the same to build up the restaurant, but they've resisted so far."

"Where's your family's restaurant?"

"In the city on Audubon Place. It's called Olympia's, for obvious reasons."

"I'll put that on my list of places to eat next time I'm in New Orleans."

"Just tell them you know me and they'll cut you a good deal."

"They'll probably charge me double, thinking that if I'm a friend of yours, I'll be trouble," Annalise teased.

Niko gave her a genuine smile. "Minx."

This was fun! In the past, when a man had flirted with her, she'd often thought of amusing retorts in kind but she'd never just blurted them out like this. She'd been too shy.

But with Niko she felt bold and confident. It was a good feeling.

"Want to sit here?" She gestured to a nearby table.

"Sure." Niko offered Annalise a hand to help her sit on the bar stool fronting the coffee bar. He probably did it without even realizing how chivalrous he was being. But Annalise didn't take the courtesy for granted.

His hand was big. Strong. Probably very nice. Still, she pretended not to notice as she climbed onto the bar stool.

As soon as he withdrew his hand she regretted not taking it. Maybe this time would have been different. After all, Niko was different.

He gave her a thoughtful look as he took the seat next to her, obviously not knowing what his personal touch would do to her. How could he know?

She'd never told anyone why she usually kept her distance. She'd never wanted to explain herself, never wanted a man to understand, until now. Maybe she should give him just enough clues that he'd know it wasn't him but her.

She swallowed. "Niko, I—"

The barista interrupted the moment and Annalise didn't know whether to feel relieved or disappointed.

She gave them the coffee-house spiel as she lined up six small cups of coffee in front of them.

"I recommend trying the samples from light roast to dark roast. Lighter is less acidic. Darker has more body." She put an icy-cold silver creamer and sugar bowl on a silver tray on the table. "Let me know if you want to try anything else on the board or if you have any questions."

Niko had lots of questions, but not for the barista. He wanted to know everything about the fascinating woman across from him. He especially wanted to know about the pain in her eyes and how to make it go away.

But by the way Annalise was avoiding looking at him, he knew this wasn't the time or the place.

He would enjoy the moment for what it was and do his best to make sure Annalise enjoyed it, too. There would be other opportunities. He would make sure of that.

After making generous use of the sugar bowl, he took his first sip and hid his wince. Coffee wasn't his favorite drink, but he would have agreed to share a bottle of absinthe if he'd had to, rather than turn down Annalise's invitation.

Annalise took a sip of first cup and grimaced.

"Not to your taste?"

"Not this one." She dumped cream and sugar into her next cup and gave it try. "Too much more of this and I'll have another restless night."

"Another?" Niko added cream to his cup, too, but hesitated before giving it another try.

"You know, Niko, I don't really like coffee. And I'm thinking you don't either. Would you rather have a nice umbrella drink instead?"

"To tell you the truth, Annalise, I'm not very fond of those either." He leaned forward, knowing he was about to either breach a barrier or end this barely budding relationship at one go. "Instead of getting ourselves into something neither of us want, let's make a pact. Truth between us and nothing less."

By the wary expression on Annalise's face Niko knew he had his answer.

"All right." She laughed—a genuine laugh from deep inside. "You were expecting a different answer, weren't you?"

"Sadly, yes. Bad past experiences."

"About that—experiences, I mean. I'll be truthful, but I also reserve the right to not answer."

"Deal." He thought of the sweepstakes ploy he'd engineered for his family and, of course, his Doctors Without Borders gig. "Everyone has a few secrets they don't want revealed."

Niko caught the barista's attention and they placed their orders—a beer for Niko and a fresh cup of tea for Annalise because she had to check back in with her P.A. before the end of office hours.

"So…" Annalise licked her lips, making Niko yearn for a taste "…want to play Twenty Questions?"

"Sure." He couldn't have refused if his life had depended on it.

"Favorite color."

"I would have said blue before I saw you today. Now it's orange. Most definitely orange."

A rosy blush crept up her face even as her eyes sparkled. She ducked her head. "Thanks."

"What's yours?"

"Mine?"

"Your favorite color?"

She grinned. "Amber. Like your eyes."

Women had complimented his eyes before, but it had never mattered. Now it mattered. *Keep it casual, Christopoulos.*

He pushed the flattering remark away. "So you want to play that way, huh? Game on, girl. What do you want in a man?"

Annalise bit her lip as she tilted her head to the side and considered. Worry made Niko's heart pound faster.

From her expression, she was taking this game way too seriously.

"Kindness. Compassion. Strength enough to stand up for those weaker than him. Enough intelligence to hold up his end of the conversation." Very deliberately, she studied him. "And muscles in all the right places."

He spread his arms wide. "You might need to check me out for that last one, Doc. A physical exam would be so much more thorough than a mere visual inspection."

As she took a sip of her tea she looked up from under her lashes. So coy yet so direct. He couldn't stop staring at how she seemed to glow from deep inside when she was happy.

"And you, Dr. Christopoulos. What makes a ladies' man like you choose one woman over another? Give me a comparison chart, no names necessary."

"Comparison chart? Right now, you're the only woman I can even bring to mind."

"You're a glib one, aren't you?"

He put his hand over his heart. "Only truth between us."

"In that case, how long have you experienced this selective amnesia, Doctor?"

"Ever since I stood behind you when we were boarding."

"What about a certain buxom Greek heiress who needed sunscreen rubbed on her back?"

Helena hadn't even entered his mind. "Merely being polite. Are you jealous?"

"Nothing to be jealous about."

"You're right. You have nothing to be jealous about." He reached over to take Annalise's hand, but she checked her watch before his fingers could graze hers.

"I need to check in with my P.A." She looked down at her activities list and pointed to the next one on the list. "Look. They've got an origami towel-folding class starting in a few minutes. Would you like to try that?"

"Towel origami? Was it something I said?"

She looked at him, long and hard. "Duty before pleasure. You know the score."

"All too well." But something in her eyes didn't ring true. He was pretty certain he was getting the brush-off.

Still, he held out his hand to help her off the bar stool.

When she took it, giving his fingers an apologetic squeeze, he felt a zing go straight to his gut. This woman was different. Special.

And he loved a challenge.

"See you tonight on top?" he called after her.

She stopped and gave him a sexy look over her shoulder. "If you're lucky."

Annalise didn't show.

Niko waited until past midnight, tensing in anticipation each time he heard footsteps coming up the metal stairs, but he was disappointed each time.

He went over and over the conversation in his head. Had he come on too strong? Shy had never been his type before Annalise. But she had seemed to enjoy their banter.

And why did it mean so much to him? Why did he feel so at a loss? Feel such rejection?

As he unlocked his cabin door, he saw the blinking light on his cabin phone. Impatiently, he followed the lengthy button-pushing instructions to retrieve the text message that scrolled across the phone's display.

Medical emergency. How about tomorrow? Ice skating after breakfast? A.

Short. Cryptic. Exactly the kind of note he'd texted his ex when he had been running late. Now he understood why she hadn't always been satisfied with his terse communication.

Niko spent too many hours staring at the ceiling, thinking about relationships old and new, telling himself he should back away from this one before he fell too deep. Then, finally, admitting to himself he might have already fallen.

As he fell asleep he made the firm, sensible decision to skip the skating date, skip the moonlight trysts, skip all further encounters with Dr. Annalise Walcott. There was no future in it. He had enough goodbyes to say at the end of this trip. No sense in adding one more.

CHAPTER SEVEN

ANNALISE STUDIED THE contents of her closet and clothes drawers. While the ice rink wasn't too cold, her body was acclimated to the tropics. Usually, for ice skating she wore thick sweats, but she opted for her slimmer-fitting yoga pants this morning. Being a little chilled was worth the fashion trade-off.

She contemplated her oversized sweatshirt advertising the cruise line. Her other option was a T-shirt, which would be too thin no matter how much better it showed off her assets.

As she pulled the sweatshirt over her head, Annalise was not oblivious to the change Niko was making on her daily habits.

They definitely had chemistry together, but it wasn't only sexual attraction but also intellectual attraction.

Annalise's mother had often told her that she was too smart for her own good. That she intimidated men and she should try to tone down the brains. While she would have if she could have, she hadn't managed to do that. But with Niko she had no need to. He challenged her mind just as she did his.

Was he the right man? Or was this simply the right time? Even before she'd met him, she had been feeling the need for a change, thus her reluctance to renew her contract and her growing interest in medical relief missions. Even her unsuccessful visit to her mother could be seen as a sign that she was ready to move on from her status quo.

The right man at the right time.

Was she ready? How long was she going to let her past hold her back?

Dark secrets. Was she prepared to look at them in the light of day? It would take a very special man to help her breach the darkness and come into the light.

Did she want Niko to be that man? Would he even want to be that man once he found out about her past?

Secrets.

Niko watched Annalise walk toward him as he stood by the skate counter, fully aware how his pulse sped up at the sight of her.

So much for all his late-night contemplation.

He had no idea where this was going, but if it was leading to something serious… He surprised himself by wishing it could. But he would never be ready for a serious relationship. He'd made his decision.

Thankfully, Annalise was safe. She had her career, too. A career that harbored no expectations of a home and children and a husband who came home every night.

"Hey," he said as she came within earshot.

"Hey back at ya."

Niko grinned at how they had fallen into sync so quickly. He could get used to this. Warning bells went off in his head. Less than three weeks. No sense in getting used to anything about her.

Still, he could enjoy her company, couldn't he? She didn't just pretend to listen when he talked. She really *did* listen. They had well-informed conversations, give and take, back and forth. Yin and yang.

How often had he been misunderstood in the past? A parade of beautiful women flashed through his mind. He had to admit he had not always based his date choice on compatibility.

But with Annalise he had both beauty and brains in one package.

The only problem was—he didn't have her at all. She was her own woman with her own life that he only got to be a part of for the next two weeks and a few days.

This trip was supposed to be about relaxing, not about feeling the pressure of the clock ticking. Why did he do this to himself?

"Ready?" She raised an eyebrow at him in challenge.

Because he couldn't resist, he answered, "Ready."

As Niko bent to lace his skates, he rubbed his thigh, an absent gesture Annalise was certain he wasn't even aware of.

"How's the leg?"

"Fine."

Although she wanted to probe deeper, she practiced great restraint and let it drop. He was entitled to his privacy, just as she was.

"I'm ready to get rid of these stitches."

"I'll take a look tomorrow."

She watched him stand on the rubber map, his ankles wobbling. As soon as she stood, he grabbed her shoulder to steady himself.

Normally, she would shy away from such contact. But this was Niko. Instead, she reached out a hand to steady him.

"You really meant it when you said you wanted

me to teach you to skate. You've never done this before?"

"Nope. Never."

"Keep your ankles firm."

"And then?"

"Then the first thing you need to learn is how to fall."

His grip tightened on her as he wobbled back and forth. "I'm thinking that lesson will come to me naturally in a very short time."

"Falling isn't inevitable."

"Except for falling in love," he quipped. Then he became very still. "At least, that's what Yiayia would say."

She was all too aware that they were avoiding each other's eyes. "That L-word can ruin a lot of friendships."

He nodded. "Then we won't let that happen, will we?"

Abruptly he sat on the bench behind him, craning up to look at her.

She sat next to him, putting them at the same height.

"Annalise?"

"Yes?"

"We can be friends, can't we? Even after this is over?"

She drew in a big breath. "Long distance? We can try. No promises, though."

He nodded. "No promises."

A group of teens rushed by, laughing and playing and reminding Annalise that life was full of fun as well as drama.

"Are we going to skate today, or hold down this bench for the rest of the morning?" she dared him.

"Let's skate." This time when he stood up he planted his feet firmly, not needing her for support.

"If you start to fall, lean back, tuck your chin in to protect your head and fall on your butt."

"Sage advice for life as well as for ice skating." He reached for her, brushing a strand of hair from her eyes. His finger lingered on the rim of her ear as he pushed the strand behind it.

The thrill made Annalise jerk away.

His lips were so close to hers she could almost taste them when he asked, "Ticklish?"

She took a step backwards, her skate catching on the rubber mat. As she windmilled her arms, he reached out to catch her.

They both lost their balance and he ended up sitting down hard on the bench with her in his lap.

Annalise jumped up.

"Sorry," she said, even though he should be the one apologizing. She hadn't been expecting that sizzling touch. She certainly hadn't asked for it either.

"I'm not."

Take it in stride, Annalise, she reminded herself. *This is flirting. This is fun. Nothing else. And nothing more.*

"Watch me." She walked in front of him. "See how I'm walking a bit forward and bending my knees?"

"Yes. I see."

The teasingly licentious tone of his voice made her grin but she didn't turn around and return it. Not this time. Too much had passed between them that needed some space.

She heard a scrape of blades once he came onto the ice, but no *kerplump*.

Turning, she skated backwards and instructed, "Just lean forward and bend your knees, like you're a superhero if you have to exaggerate it, until you get your balance."

Niko's black hair fell forward into his eyes, making Annalise think about how he could be her Clark Kent any day. Just not today. Too much, too soon.

Then again, this trip wasn't going to last forever.

Niko closed his eyes and took a breath, apparently finding his balance because when he opened them he said, "I'm ready."

And then he skated like he'd been born on the ice, taking long, sure strides and handling the corners with no problems for several laps.

He ran into the wall of the rink to stop.

He looked back over his shoulder at her. "Not graceful but effective."

Showing off a little, she demonstrated a hockey-style stop.

He raised an eyebrow. "Isn't there an easier way?"

"See the cleats on the blade? Drag your toe. They'll catch and slow you down until you stop."

He tried stopping a few times and then said, "Now I'm ready to do that thing you did when you turned around to skate backwards."

"Okay. Changing direction is best done while you're moving, not standing still."

She skated away from him, then crossed her feet and executed a smooth turn so that she faced him, skating backwards. It had taken her many hours of practice to be able to change direction so smoothly.

"Be patient with yourself if you don't get it right the first time."

"I'm not big on patience."

She skated towards him, turning again when she drew even with him. "I've sensed that about you."

Niko took a couple of strides, then crossed his feet, doing a complete circle instead of a half-one.

"It takes practice." Annalise turned back and forth a half dozen times in as many strides, enjoying what she was doing as much as flaunting her skills.

Niko frowned down at her feet, then nodded and gave it a try. Of course, he picked up the technique on the second pass. Was there anything this man couldn't do?

He dragged a toe, ending up a few inches from her, close enough she could see the golden flecks in his eyes. "Now that I've done it, I don't understand the appeal of going round in circles. Maybe speed skating or doing those dangerous moves and jumps they do on television would make it more exciting." He skated backwards to Annalise's forwards.

"Always the extremes for you, isn't it, Niko?"

He looked sad. "It's when I feel most alive."

But that wasn't precisely true. Not anymore. He felt the same thrilling awareness of existence whenever he was with Annalise.

It wasn't a revelation he was happy to discover. But he couldn't make a clean break of it. Finding an excuse to prolong this, he scratched at his thigh through his shorts. "No office hours today, huh?"

"Impatient man." Her smile was strained as she sat on the bench to unlace her skates.

Niko sat next to her, though not as close as he had before. Was there something more behind her bantering exasperation? He shouldn't want there to be more.

"Come by tomorrow morning and I'll take a look."

Tomorrow morning. Niko wanted to ask about tonight.

"Maybe I could just borrow a pair of scissors and tweezers." He gave her a practiced grin as he kicked off his skate. "I'm ready to try the water slides."

"You can always stop in and visit my P.A."

Niko thought about that, thought about how that was a very sound solution, then thought about how he yearned to feel Annalise's warm hand on his leg, gently tending to him. He decided he could put off the water slides until tomorrow.

He lined up his skates, one next to the other, and slipped into his tennis shoes, wiggling his toes at the familiar comfortable fit.

"See you then—if not tonight?"

"Tomorrow, for sure. Tonight?" She bent to unlace her second skate, effectively hiding her face behind her hair. "Maybe."

He wanted to ask what he could to do convince her, to insist. To make her commit.

Which would call for commitment on his part, too.

He checked his watch. "Family calls. I need to check on Sophie."

"Okay."

"See you then," Niko said again, restraining himself from clearing up the ambiguity. These things happened in their own time. If only he had that much time.

He grabbed both pairs of skates and headed for the counter to turn them in.

He couldn't help watching her as she walked away, her bottom perfectly defined in those form-fitting yoga pants beneath that huge sweatshirt. He'd bet each of those perfect butt cheeks would fit perfectly in his hands. How wise was he to want to prove himself right?

After filling the rest of her morning with grueling, hot yoga then a long swim in the pool after lunch, along with a trip to the video arcade to play a big-screen version of tennis, and a couple of miles on the treadmill instead of supper, Annalise should have been dropping from exhaustion. Instead, she found herself climbing the three sets of stairs to the top deck, a cup of hot decaf tea in her hand, anticipation in her heart.

The deck was deserted.

Annalise almost turned around and left but stopped herself in mid-step. What was she doing? A cup of tea on the top deck had been her habit ever since she'd started sailing on this ship. After all the cruises she'd worked, why would she let one man on one cruise change a tradition that gave her so much pleasure?

Hazy memories of the pleasures her dream lover had almost given her had her sloshing tea over the rim of her cup. It was a dream she would welcome again.

As she would welcome the man behind the dream?

Today, for the first time since she'd signed her first contract, the huge ship seemed too small. Like her P.A. had said, Annalise was a legend in the cruise line's history for her longevity of employment. Most people got tired of running from whatever it was, or found what they were running towards, after a few seasons of ship work. But she'd always been slow to make a change, hanging onto stability, to security.

Her yoga instructor would say that without change there was no growth. And without growth, death. At least in spirit.

Wasn't that what had happened to her own mother so many years ago?

Annalise was not like her mother. But, then, flirting with a man didn't mean selling her soul to him. That's not what a relationship, or even a casual encounter, had to be.

She had established her professional life on her own terms. She could certainly establish her love life on her own terms, too.

Right before the sun made its nightly plunge into the ocean, she heard Niko running up the steps.

"I didn't miss it, did I?"

"Even the sunset waits on Niko Christopoulos."

She'd expected that to elicit a smile or even a laugh from him. Instead, he settled down next to her, twisted the top off one of the two beers he held and saluted the pink and yellow horizon.

"To peace of mind." Although the strangle hold he had on the neck of his beer bottle told a different story.

She raised her tea cup in solidarity. "To peace of mind."

Niko lay back on the lounger with the last of the

sun's rays casting shadows over his face, making him look tired.

She wanted to make it all better but they didn't have that kind of relationship. Silence was the best she could do.

As they lay within arm's reach of each other, attraction snapping between them like heat lightning, Annalise wondered how this would end.

CHAPTER EIGHT

NIKO WAS THE first one in her office. It was easy to do since he'd been up since before dawn. In fact, he wasn't sure he'd slept at all.

Annalise had been too much on his mind.

He hadn't spent a sleepless night over a woman in…in longer than he could remember.

Annalise bit her bottom lip, a worried line appearing between her eyebrows. "That knife could have sliced across your throat as easily as it cut into your thigh."

"Lots of things could happen that never do."

"You're one of the lucky ones. You have a family that cares. You could have died and they wouldn't have even known why. Closure heals a lot of hurts."

But acknowledging that something fatal could happen meant dealing with the emotions associated with that nebulous something. He didn't do family drama very well. "I'm going to tell them as soon as the time is right."

Niko felt Annalise's hand burning on his thigh. Her touch set him on fire. He couldn't deny it.

Just as he couldn't deny that he was a man of flesh and blood. If this had been more serious, if he had died, his family would never have understood. He would never have had the opportunity to explain. He owed them more than that.

Annalise was right. Soon. As soon as the opportunity presented itself.

Like that was ever going to happen.

Niko pushed that thought away, determined to squeeze every ounce of enjoyment out of this trip. He had almost two weeks left and he would make the most of them.

After Annalise confirmed that Niko's knife wound was healing well enough, he sat on the exam table and picked out his own stitches, using the tweezers and scissors Annalise lent him as she stood, propped against the wall, watching him.

She'd offered. He could have accepted. But her hand on his thigh would have led to an embarrassing situation that his baggy board shorts couldn't have hidden.

He looked up at her from under thick, dark lashes. "Are you as good at climbing the rock wall as you are at ice skating?"

She arched a brow at him. "Better."

"As soon as I'm done here, then, want to race?"

"I don't know. I might be taking unfair advantage." Annalise frowned as Niko tugged on one of the stitches to get it loose. "Living on this ship, I've climbed that wall a thousand times at least. And I've scaled real rocks, too."

"Yeah? When?"

"Before I was hired by the cruise line, I signed up for the emergency medicine residency swap program. So I gave New Mexico's emergency medicine program a try. I learned to climb there."

"You're just full of surprises."

She shrugged. "In New Orleans, I'd always lived around three feet below sea level in the inner city. I thought I'd try different terrain for a while."

"What did you think of it?" Field medicine wasn't for most doctors.

"I loved everything about it. The mountains. The desert. It was like the elements dared me and I was determined to win."

"Sweet Annalise in those rugged conditions. I've noticed you've got a competitive edge." The need to beat the odds was the attitude it took to be a good field doctor. More and more, he was learning there was more to Annalise than he'd thought at first glance. Although the first glance had been rather thrilling, too.

"You're doing it again." She rubbed at her cheek. "You're staring at me like I've got something on my face."

"Sorry. I must be losing my touch. That's supposed to be my intensely interested look. Obviously, I need to work on it."

"Honesty?"

"Honesty." He crossed his heart and held up his fingers like a scout. "When you smile like that, I can't help but stare."

She laughed, shaking her head at his compliment, not taking him seriously. "You and your flattery."

While he'd totally meant the compliment, he liked it that she wasn't too taken in by it. Annalise definitely stood on her own two feet.

"But a beautiful woman deserves beautiful compliments."

"Pretty is as pretty does." She gave him a sideways look. "You're good looking. Does that make you a better person?"

Her question, delivered quick and solid, caught Niko by surprise. "Of course not."

"Remember that next time you're throwing around random compliments."

Niko thought of the sinking feeling he always got when he thought a woman was more interested in his appeal as an arm ornament than as a person. "Yes, ma'am, I will."

He flexed his leg, watching the healed skin hold true. "If you were in the emergency response residency program, I'm guessing you specialized in emergency medicine. So how did you end up here?"

"I applied for a couple of positions that would have set me up for emergency rescue work." She swept her arm around the exam room. "I was seduced by the glamour of all this."

He looked around in appreciation, catching a glimpse of the ocean out the high transom window. "It's a nice gig."

"I've had it for a while. And it puts me in the position of being an excellent rock-wall climber. Ready to lose to a girl?"

"Winner gets a back rub!" Niko didn't know why he'd said that. When he saw the shocked look in Annalise's eyes, he almost awkwardly retracted the prize.

But then she blinked and said, "You're on," and he was glad after all. Regardless of who made it to the top first, he was a winner.

And that's exactly what he was feeling, clinging to the wall as he looked up and over at Annalise's ankle, up to her calf, to her thigh and her wonderfully perfect butt.

"Hey, Uncle Niko, are you going to let a girl beat you?"

Why had he thought he was going to do this without an audience of family members?

The harness straps cut him in places where he'd rather not feel that kind of pain. To get some relief, Niko found the next toehold and pushed upwards. Because he was taller than she was, now he was even with her.

She looked over and met his eyes. "You haven't won yet, Christopoulos."

His fingers touched a plastic thing bolted onto the fake rock and he dug the tips of his fingers around the edge to pull himself up.

At the same time Annalise reached for the same plastic thing, covering his hand with hers.

"Oh!" She jerked her hand back. So he wasn't the only one that felt the heat when they touched.

Her eyes went wide as she swung her arm wildly, off balance. Then down she went on her guide rope. She fell at least halfway before the rope latch stopped her.

By the surprised but happy grin on her face she was fine.

Niko thought for a moment. He could slide down

now, too, but that would mean no winner. And no winner would mean no back rub.

He gave her a wry look. "I like my massages with warm oil," he said, just loud enough for her to hear.

"You haven't made it yet." She swung back to face the wall, scrambled for a plastic thing and began climbing much faster than she'd climbed earlier, making him realize she'd been holding back and pacing herself to him.

The competitive spirit kicked in full force. Niko felt around with his foot, reached outside his comfort zone and found the toehold he was looking for. His healing leg quivered from fatigue as he willed muscle and sinew to lift.

It was a stretch but he could almost reach the next—

And then he was falling, falling, with his stomach flipping until the harness jerked him to a halt.

"Ow." The harness did unkind things to him. Good thing he hadn't planned on having kids.

Annalise paused her climb to look down at him as he dangled a few feet from the floor.

"You okay?"

"Just singing soprano now."

She gave him a wink then covered the last four

feet of wall as if she were a spider. With great aplomb she rang the bell at the top.

"For form's sake," she called down to him as she planted her feet and descended in graceful hops as if she'd been born on the mountains instead of on the flat, soggy soil of New Orleans.

Niko worked at setting his own feet and pushing against the wall, descending until he finally touched the deck.

Annalise was only two hops ahead of him. By the time he'd unbuckled his harness, she had hers off, too.

Before the Christopoulos clan could totally engulf them, he leaned over close. With any other woman, he would be suggesting his room, but that didn't feel right with Annalise. She needed more finesse. And he was pleased to be the one to give her what she needed. Instead, he asked, "Tonight on deck?"

She nodded, adding, "I like my oil to smell like lavender."

And then she was gone, wading through his brothers and nephews and sisters-in-law and nieces as they gathered around to snap pictures and pat him on the back and tease him as only a brother could about his loss to a girl.

As he anticipated the evening activities, he

couldn't help but grin. This was no loss. In fact, it was a pretty big win in his book.

Annalise made her way up to the top deck with equal parts of anticipation and trepidation. Maybe she should have let him win? Then she would have been more in control, touching him instead of him touching her.

Stop it, Annalise. It's just a back rub in public.

She wore her swimsuit underneath her shirt and shorts. She'd thought long and hard about what to wear, giving it much more consideration than the situation merited.

Should he really go through the trouble of finding lavender oil, the modest one-piece exposed her shoulders and back and was easily washable.

If this back-rub thing started to become more than fun and games… Every time she imagined how his hands would feel, her mind skittered away.

As she rounded the corner, she saw he was already there on his favorite chair.

"Hey." His voice reached that place deep within her that her mind had been avoiding thinking about.

She rubbed her hands down her arms to rub away the prickles that danced along her skin.

She swallowed. "Hey back at ya." It was throaty, husky and entirely not what she had intended.

He had her chair decked out with a couple of thick towels and a bottle of oil with an expensive label she recognized from the spa on deck three.

He stood and indicated the lounge chair. "Madam, your masseur awaits your pleasure." With an exaggerated leer he rubbed his hands together then cracked his knuckles.

Before she could lose her nerve, she whipped off her top. "Just remember, you're a cabana boy tonight, not a chiropractor."

She thought about lying prone, but that seemed too intimate so she straddled the lounger instead. "So I can watch the sunset," she explained. *So I won't feel so vulnerable,* she admitted to herself.

"Okay." He swung his leg over to straddle the lounger behind her, thigh to thigh. "I like exploring new positions."

Annalise was too busy reacting to the sizzle along her nerve endings to think of a retort. *I want this,* she reminded herself.

At the first touch of his palms on her shoulders, her apprehension made her shiver.

"Relax," he crooned into her ear, which made her feel anything but relaxed.

His hands, slick with fragrant oil, slid along her

shoulders until this thumbs found the knot at the base of her neck. With the right amount of firmness and gentleness, he made circular motions to get her shoulders to loosen.

Annalise tried to concentrate on the sunset instead of the man who sat inches behind her.

His hands stilled. "Okay?"

She wanted to be okay. With every cell of her body she wanted to want this, to enjoy this, to want more.

"Annalise?" It was a question wrapped in a worry.

A noisy crowd of five people scrambled onto the deck she'd foolishly begun to think of as their private nirvana.

She had a sinking feeling at the relief she felt to be interrupted.

"I— We..." What should she say? Sorry? Maybe next time? I wish things could be different?

"Look at me!" One of the intruders stood at the rail and held out her arms. "It's like I'm flying."

The others gave it a try, cackling with laughter and spilling drinks in the process.

Niko dropped his hands and blew out a sigh as Annalise leaned forward to grab for her shirt.

She pulled it on, grimacing when the back stuck to the oil on her skin.

Niko sat motionless behind her. She couldn't even feel him breathe.

Without a glance she got up and headed downstairs, down to her cabin with no windows, down to her dark little hidey-hole that kept the world locked out—but kept her locked in.

For the first time in years she cried into her pillow. Long, ragged, ugly sobs for all that had happened to her and who she wanted to be.

With her throat too swollen and sore to cry anymore, she made up her mind. She would not be a victim for the rest of her life.

Many hours later, as she lay in bed, reliving the scene over and over again, she kept up her litany, praying it wasn't falling on deaf ears. *Please. Another chance.*

CHAPTER NINE

NOT ALL PRAYERS were answered.

Her patient load was extraordinarily heavy with barely breathing room. Between shifts, Annalise tried to casually run into Niko but could never find him. She even made a point to look for the Christopoulos clan at their family dinner, even though she dreaded facing the lot of them. All that family happiness only contrasted with her own sad situation, reminding her how different she and Niko were. But her need for Niko overcame her unease.

She found out from their waiter that her courage was for naught. Apparently, they'd all decided to forgo formal dining in favor of an early picnic by the wave pool.

That evening, she sat alone on the top deck, watching a sunset obscured by stormclouds. Today was only the beginning of much rougher seas ahead.

Was Niko avoiding her? Of course he was. She

couldn't blame him. He must think her the most fickle female on the planet.

But the next evening found her on the top deck once again, hoping. Praying.

After all, what better did she have do to and where better did she have to go?

Niko called himself all kinds of a fool as he climbed the stairs to the top deck. Some things just weren't meant to be so why was he trying so hard?

Because he couldn't get her out of his head.

He clenched his fists, remembering the feel of her skin under his palms. The energy that radiated through her into him made him feel so buzzed, so alive.

But she could turn it off faster than any woman he'd ever met. Maybe it was his imagination, but when she looked at him he thought he saw a wistfulness in her eyes. And he wanted to—had to—give her whatever it was she wanted. *Because he wouldn't be complete until she was.*

Niko rubbed at his eyes, trying to rub away that fanciful thought. With any other woman he would have walked away by now. But there was something—something that had him coming back to her.

He didn't know if that something was in her or in

him. All he knew was that he was climbing these stairs because he couldn't think of any other place he would be okay about being in right now.

"Hey," she offered cautiously.

"Hey back at you." He set down between them the two cups of hot tea he'd brought up.

"Busy morning?" he asked.

"And booked until late afternoon, too. They come in—"

"Waves." He finished her sentence for her. "It happens that way, doesn't it? Biorhythms or something."

"I always blame it on moon phases." The conversation felt stilted, but at least they were talking.

She watched him add three packets of sugar to his tea. "Not sweet enough?"

He held up the cup. "Bitter. It steeped too long. But enough sweetener can fix anything."

Could she be fixed with enough sweetener? She hoped so. "I heard the Christopoulos boys closed the bar down last night." She'd heard it from Brandy at yoga that morning. She'd also heard Niko had turned down quite a few offers of female company before moving to the sports section of the bar to watch football with his brothers instead.

"We won." He hoisted his cup. "Go, Tigers. But,

then, I think I cheered them on one too many times last night."

She grinned at his hesitant hurrah. "You're on vacation. You're supposed to be having fun."

Vacation. The fun wouldn't last for ever. And hers might be over before it even began if she didn't take action.

"I've had fun. I've especially enjoyed the ship's medical services. The cruise line employs a very fine doctor."

"Compliment accepted." She sipped her tea.

"I have to admit, though, while I've enjoyed my time aboard ship, I'll be glad to make our first port. I didn't realize these transatlantic cruises had so much sea time up front." Niko took a sip of tea and winced. "Only two more days, right?"

"Yes. Two more days until our first port of call, Isle de Paridisio."

"You've been there?"

"A few times."

He took a sip of tea. "At least I've got it drinkable."

"You could have always got another cup."

"I like this one just fine." He stared out at the ocean. "I know my family is a handful, but we would love to have you join us."

This was the opportunity she'd asked for. The

one she'd prayed for. A second chance for her. She needed this so much. Such a double-edged sword.

"I'm sorry. I can't." Turning him down was one of the hardest decisions she'd ever made.

The ill and injured of Isle de Paridisio needed her more.

The cruise line fully supported staff volunteering at the various ports of call, often matching private donations and giving away tons of food to the shelters.

Annalise always offered her assistance to any of the medical clinics along the cruise ship's routes. So many of these tropical paradises had beautiful tourist resorts as a thin veneer over the destitution of the rest of the island.

During their stopover at Isle de Paradisio, the youth directors would visit a local orphanage to donate books and clothing and the kitchen chefs would donate food. Other staff would help, too.

Annalise would head to the refugee camp. So many refugees traversed the Mediterranean, making it only this far, with nothing but their lives to call their own.

She had medicine to deliver, donated by New Orleans charities, and she would lend a hand where she could while she was on the island.

The beeper on her hip buzzed. She squinted in

the failing light to read the code, seeing that it signaled an immediate emergency.

"I've got to go."

"Of course. Duty calls. Been there. Done that." His mouth twisted into a wry smile. "Maybe later."

"Wake up, sweetie. Wake up for Yiayia." Hearing those ominous words float down the hallway of the medical suite, Annalise's heart sank like a stone and she picked up her fast walk to an all-out run.

There was Sophie, lying limp in her Uncle Stephen's arms.

Her other uncle, all her aunts and her cousins surrounded her. If love could fix her, she would be the healthiest little girl on the planet. Sadly, juvenile diabetes had no cure.

Her clothes were urine-soaked. Her little arm felt cold and clammy and her breathing was so slow as to be barely detectable.

"Did she vomit?"

The whole family started talking at once, but the general gist was that they didn't think so.

Annalise spotted Marcus. "Get your Uncle Niko. He's on the upper foredeck."

She would need him to run interference with his family as she helped the little girl.

"Bring her in," she directed Stephen, and pointed to the nearest exam table. "Where's her meter?"

Phoebe pulled it from her tote along with the notebook.

Annalise pricked Sophie's finger and the meter evaluated Sophie's blood-sugar level.

It was dangerously high.

Sophie's endocrinologist had warned Annalise that trying to balance blood sugar was more of a gut feeling than an exact formula. Drawing on her healer's instinct, Annalise grabbed a vial of fast-acting insulin and checked the charts. She filled a syringe conservatively and gave Sophie the injection. Now the wait.

Meanwhile, she wrapped a rubber tourniquet around Sophie's arm, trying to find a vein so she could draw a blood sample from her dehydrated little body.

Vaguely, she was aware of Niko herding out his well-meaning family members.

"Find out what happened," Annalise threw over her shoulder as she prepared to prick the vein.

Sophie fluttered her eyelids and feebly tried to move her arm away. "No. Don't."

It was a sleepy response, but still a response.

"Be brave, little one," Annalise murmured.

Niko's big, strong hand came into view, gently holding Sophie's tiny arm still.

Sophie opened her eyes. "Uncle Niko?"

"I'm here for you, Sophie."

"I'm taking this to the lab. Stay with her, okay?" Annalise put the sample in the analyzer then rejoined them while the machine did its work.

Sophie's spark of defiance had been short-lived as she now lay still once again.

"What's the scoop, Niko?"

"Her aunt had given her permission to get a banana from the fruit bar. Apparently, Sophie figured out how to use the ice-cream machine next to it by herself. A helpful passenger boosted her up when she was too short to reach it. That inspired a binge. One of her cousins tattled and they found Sophie hiding under a dining-room table with a tray full of cookies and donuts and brownies. By the time they found her, it was too late to prevent this."

She handed Niko a water bottle. "Get her to drink as much as you can."

Annalise checked her watch. Almost twenty minutes.

This time Sophie protested the meter prick, which was as good a sign of her recovery as the blood-sugar level, which was slowly edging downwards. She gave Sophie and Niko a reassuring smile. "We're getting there."

The lab analyzer beeped and Annalise read the results.

Showing them to Niko, she pointed to the potassium levels. "Looks like we're okay here."

"Thank God." Niko bent down and placed a kiss on his niece's forehead. "I should have been there. I promised my brother I would watch over her."

"No, Niko. Stop it." Annalise hesitated, then touched his shoulder. "Your family is saying the same thing. But they're only human. Do you blame them?"

"Of course not."

"Then don't blame yourself either."

He scrubbed his hand through his hair. "Little kids should be able to sneak an occasional ice-cream cone. They shouldn't have to get injections three times a day the rest of their lives. It's not fair."

"You, of all people, with all you've seen, all you've done, know that life's not fair and bad things happen. We do what we can to pick up the pieces and go on."

Niko looked into her eyes, searching—for what? Sincerity? Truth? She had that in spades.

Acceptance that they had to make peace with

the unfairness of the world? No. She couldn't give him that.

"You understand, don't you?" He ran his finger down her cheek. "You understand the frustration of not being able to make everything all right."

She nodded. "I understand."

On the table, Sophie stirred. Her face screwed up in a scowl. "I'm wet. Who threw water on me?" She sniffed. "Somebody peed on me."

Niko shook his head. "You had an uh-oh, little one."

"I'm not a baby. I don't wet my pants." But the embarrassment in her face showed she understood that she had. To cover up, she pawed at the bandage taped to her arm, where Annalise had taken her blood sample. "This hurts."

Niko and Annalise both grinned at her irritability, a good sign of her recovery.

Niko raised an eyebrow at her. "This happened because of the ice cream and the cookies and the donuts, Sophie." He said it gently but firmly.

Annalise knew him well enough to know it was breaking his heart to deliver this lesson.

"But Phillip got some."

"You have to be more careful than Phillip. He doesn't get sick when he eats too much sugary food but you do."

"It's not fair."

Niko shrugged, a studied, calculated movement by the stiffness of his shoulders. "But that's the way it is."

Annalise did one more blood-sugar test, pricking Sophie's finger with the meter before she could protest. As Sophie glared at her, Annalise read the meter and found the level becoming more satisfactory.

She documented everything in Sophie's notebook and then wrote down her instructions. "We should be seeing normal readings in about another hour and a half. If not, call me. I'd do a check every hour for the next three hours or so. Then every two hours so both of you can get some sleep. Watch for it to swing. Going too low can look like sleep and be a coma instead. But, then, you know that, right?"

"It's different when the patient is family." Niko rubbed his hand across his face. "I appreciate your instructions. They help me keep my head on straight."

Not having family to speak of, Annalise wouldn't know that. "Call me if the levels are out of this range."

She wrote down the numbers in the notebook. "I can't recommend sleeping in. Keep her on her morning schedule of insulin and breakfast. Maybe a nap during the day. Come and see me tomorrow afternoon and we'll do a blood test to double-check that potassium level. Until then, no bananas and no tomatoes." She made herself look into Sophie's sad, angry eyes. "And no ice cream or cookies or brownies."

As tears welled in Sophie's eyes, Annalise steeled herself to keep from joining her. Niko put his hand on Annalise's shoulder and squeezed, comforting her.

Life was unfair but she would do what she could when she could. Perhaps someday she would learn to be content with that.

Until then it was nice to know that someone in the world understood.

CHAPTER TEN

IT HAD BEEN a long, sleepless night.

After assuring himself that Sophie's blood sugar had stabilized and that she had more than enough family members surrounding her, Niko spent the morning drifting in and out of sleep on deck.

Helena kept him company. Or rather she used him to keep a would-be paparazzo at bay. Somehow the man had figured out who Helena's rich ex-husband was and had been trying to interview her about their divorce ever since last night.

Niko didn't mind. Helena was comfortable with long silences. When they did converse, she was intelligent and well read. Her ex was a fool and he told her so.

And when the waves picked up, the nosy man, along with most of the passengers, retired to the interior of the ship, where the rocking didn't seem as pronounced if they couldn't see the splash.

Which left Niko pleasantly alone except for Helena but left Annalise incredibly busy. Which might be just as well.

They had shared moments, special moments that came from deep inside him, when she'd asked about his work with Doctors Without Borders, when they'd talked of his childhood and how important his family was to him, when they'd taken care of Sophie.

But maybe those moments had only been precious to him. Looking back, Niko realized that Annalise had dodged any questions about her own life before she'd become a cruise ship doctor. Had he forgotten his own rule? The one about shipboard romances?

When this cruise was over, so would be their relationship. Serious relationship and career choice didn't fit in the same sentence for him. Yet Annalise was not a woman to be taken lightly.

"You are frowning, *filo mu*." Helena adjusted her hat brim against the sun.

Filo mu. My friend. He knew for certain Helena would be his friend only until they docked and he was fine with that. Many people passed in and out of his life. Many more would come and go in the future.

But the thought of never seeing Annalise again—

that was giving him a bit of heartburn and he wasn't sure what medicine to take that would offer relief.

Annalise had checked on Sophie throughout the day as often as she could. The child was resilient, as most children were. It helped that her young cousins treated her no differently than each other, even though the older family members tended to hover into the late afternoon.

If only the other passengers were so hardy. The waves and swells had picked up that afternoon as a storm moved in. Annalise and her colleagues had been handing out motion-sickness patches as fast as they could complete the examination. The patches took a while to work, though. Too little too late for most of the passengers.

The invitation to the captain's table tonight didn't surprise her. With this weather, he had probably received several cancellations.

Annalise wondered who she would be dining with this evening. In the mood she was in, anything was better than eating alone. She was having a hard time keeping her mind off Niko and that Greek woman he'd glued himself to all afternoon.

Jealousy, especially unjust jealousy, was an ugly

lump in her stomach she had never expected to experience.

In front of the mirror, she braced to keep from swaying with the rocking of the ship as she tried to arrange her hair. Ponytails swirled into ballerina buns were so much easier than this layered cut.

After twenty minutes of failure, she gave up on pinning the loose strands that drifted down and let them wisp around her neckline *au naturel*. She swiped on another coat of lip gloss since she'd eaten off her earlier application while trying to style her hair.

Mentally she reviewed the cases that had come through her office that day. The Christopoulos family seemed to be of robust stock, Sophie's diabetes notwithstanding. Not one family member had come to see her for seasickness.

A man like Niko wouldn't let a little thing like ocean motion interfere with his game plan. When she'd taken a quick break on deck to breathe in the fresh air, she'd seen him cozied up to that Greek heiress from Texas looking like he was her personal bodyguard.

Or maybe she had that backwards. The woman certainly looked like she wanted to guard Niko's body, keeping it all for herself. And Niko didn't appear to mind at all.

Annalise thought they'd shared something special—something unique just between the two of them all those evenings on deck. Then, the second she'd had to work, Niko had found another woman to tell his soulful tales to. Would any woman do for him or had that big-bosomed Greek goddess been able to give him something more than she could?

In the mirror, her cheeks were blotchy red. Time to take a reality check. The truth was, even though Niko had trusted her with his most precious secrets, she'd backed away whenever he'd tried to understand her. She'd shut down, just like she always did whenever anyone wanted to get close.

Annalise added more powder to her flushed cheeks then adjusted her cleavage, plumping it up to make more of it. She might not have as much going for her as the goddess, but she would make the most of what she had. And if she happened to run into Niko tonight...

What? What would she do if she happened to run into him? Promise not to leave so abruptly when the talk turned personal? Promise...?

That was the kicker. She could make no promises.

To the empty room, she said, "Who said anything about promises, Annalise? What's wrong with a little fun? No commitment required?"

Saying it aloud sounded bold and brave and beautiful, all the things she wanted to be, right? She would *not* continue to be haunted by a past that had been out of her control. She *would* live a normal life, a life that included a healthy relationship with a man.

She would look for opportunities. If not with Niko then with someone else.

That affirmation felt flat and uneasy. Try as she may, Annalise couldn't envision anyone other than Niko in her bed.

She looked at herself in the full-length mirror, reached up to adjust her halter-topped emerald-green dress for better coverage, then made herself drop her hand.

She was no more exposed than any other woman. She would hold up her head and be proud.

Niko twitched in his tuxedo as he was seated next to Helena at the captain's table. He'd dressed up for Yiayia but there she sat, across the room at a table for two. He would have to check out the little old man she was leaning so close to as they laughed together.

But now he apparently had a rich Greek heiress from Texas to entertain. He'd bet his passport his grandmother had had something to do with it.

The captain made the introductions. Mr. and Mrs. Smith, who were celebrating Mrs. Smith's seventy-fifth birthday. The ship's entertainment director. And Helena Grubbs.

"It's Artino now," she gracefully corrected him. "I'm going back to my maiden name."

"Helena. Always a pleasure." Niko murmured the polite response but ignored the hopeful question in her eyes. No. He wasn't interested.

The twins were right. She was his type. So why wasn't he more enamored of her when her big brown eyes freely offered so many possibilities? Because there was no spark. Only one woman on this ship held his interest. If only the feeling had been mutual.

"We keep running into each other," she said. "Destiny?"

He'd thought she knew where he stood. He hadn't been sending mixed messages, had he? Looking her straight in the eye, he made his intentions as clear as he could. "Maybe you're the sister I never had."

By the dimming of her expression, he saw that she finally understood.

"How about being my friend? A girl can't have too many of them, can she?" Clearly disappointed, she turned away to focus her attention on Mr. Smith.

Niko glared at his grandmother, who had put them in this awkward position, but she was too intent on the man across from her to notice.

"Is anything wrong, Mr. Christopoulos?" the captain asked.

"Nothing. I've just never seen my grandmother dine with another gentleman before."

"Don't worry. He's one of our regulars, a widower. He makes trips with us several times a year," the entertainment director reassured him.

Mrs. Smith nodded knowingly from across the table set for seven. "Running from loneliness." She patted the arm of a man seated next to her. "Thankfully, I ran into the arms of a man who promises me I'll never be lonely again."

Niko felt the emptiness of the unoccupied chair next to him.

Then he saw her heading toward them. Immediately, he stood. How could he not in the presence of such beauty?

The captain made the introductions. "Dr. Niko Christopoulos, I think you might know our ship's doctor, Annalise Walcott."

"I've had the pleasure." On impulse, he reached for her hand. Surprisingly, she held it out to him.

He carried it to his lips, breathing in the scent of lavender lotion and Annalise.

As he pulled out her chair for her he had the strongest urge to whisper in her ear and tell her how stunning she looked but he wasn't sure how she'd take it, especially in front of the captain.

"Sorry to be late," she apologized to the captain and the table at large.

"Nonsense. I know your afternoon has been busy." The captain introduced her to the couple across from her. Mr. Smith might be elderly, but he wasn't too old to appreciate Annalise's cleavage.

Niko wanted to cover her with his coat or maybe the tablecloth.

"What?" Under cover of passing the bread, Annalise asked him, "Is something wrong?"

Rein it in, Christopoulos, he told himself. "No. Nothing." He forced a smile that strained his jaw muscles.

She lifted her eyebrow, not taken in by his pseudo-civility. "Where is your family?"

"I had expected to meet them here." He nodded toward this grandmother's table. "Yiayia tells me that Stephen and Phoebe are dining alone in their room while the twins watch over the little ones in the family suite. My other brother and his wife had a casual supper earlier and are on the deck, counting stars."

The no longer lonely Mrs. Smith leaned toward them. "Such a romantic set of brothers. Does it run in the family?"

Niko could feel himself blushing under her scrutiny.

"Yes, it does." Annalise answered for him. "I've seen him in action."

"And perhaps benefitted from his seductive side?" Mrs. Smith teased.

Annalise busied herself with buttering her bread instead of answering.

Thankfully, the captain chose that moment to make a toast—most probably to save his ship's doctor from the awkward moment. "To those who love the sea!"

Obediently, they all raised their glasses. The waiters followed up the toast by presenting plates of steak and stuffed crab for each guest.

Helena, seated next to the captain, had become incredibly chatty with him, requiring no conversation from him. Besides, they'd run out of things to say early in the afternoon. Funny, thought Niko, how he and Annalise had never run out of things to talk about, even though they'd spent hours together over the last few days.

For some reason, though, the discussions they usually shared seem too intimate to have at a table full of people. Not the subject matter, although the kind of medical discussion they had would probably bore the rest of the guests, but the conversations themselves.

The entertainment director was gifted in small talk, keeping the Smiths amused with funny tales of previous cruises, while they countered with narratives of their grandchildren. All parties involved seemed to be pleased to have new ears to listen to their old stories.

Conversation flowed around Niko and Annalise, leaving them in a cocoon of silence.

Annalise seemed to be lost in thought and he respected her enough to leave her to it as she picked at her food. Was it too much to hope she felt the same way he did about their private conversations? Or had she just had a long day and needed some down time? Either way, he was content enough to sit beside her. He didn't need any other stimulation. Not that he would turn it down if more were offered.

As they were served dessert, the entertainment director interrupted their quiet contemplation.

"Annalise, I hate to ask it of you, but the weather forecast doesn't look great tomorrow. Calm seas but rain. We'll need to have more activities below deck. Do you think you could participate in a staff talent show?"

It was an activity Annalise had never minded helping with before. Dressing up in costume, being someone else for a little while, was always a kick. But sitting next to Niko, she felt shy.

Taking a big bite of strawberry pie bought her some time.

"What's your talent, dear?" Mrs. Smith asked.

"I sing a little."

"She's got a voice that will rival any rock goddess," the captain bragged. "We've got outstanding talent on this ship."

She wiped her mouth with her napkin. Hadn't she learned a long time ago that the best way to face her fear was head on? "I'll be glad to, Captain. Dr. Christopoulos used to sing in a rock band. Want to join in, Niko?"

Before he even thought about it, Niko agreed. What was it about Annalise that called forth in him the need to make her smile at him?

Not only did she smile with those luscious lips, she smiled with her eyes. Sparkling in the way they were, those green eyes made him feel like he'd just fulfilled her greatest fantasy. Or maybe that's what he read in them because that's what he wanted to see.

Because as soon as the spark had come, it went out, leaving her eyes smoky and obscure.

And leaving Niko feeling chilled. What was it about this woman who blew hot and cold? Was it him?

He turned to Helena on his other side and flashed her a questioning smile. She flashed back, reassuring him she was okay—then put her hand on his shoulder.

"I think I'll skip dessert. It's not good to rumba on a full stomach and the captain has promised me he's quite an enthusiastic dancer."

The captain pushed back his chair, almost knocking it over. "Ladies. Gentlemen. It was a pleasure."

He pulled out Helena's chair. "Madam."

"It's mademoiselle." She took his hand and they were gone.

What would Annalise feel like in his arms? Niko wondered. "Do you rumba?"

"No. But thank you." She gave him a sideways glance. "Do you?"

He took a breath. "I'm not too bad at it. I could teach you. Or if you prefer ballroom dancing, isn't there a big band playing somewhere?"

Mrs. Smith nodded. "Yes, on the aft deck."

Annalise gave him a probing look. "You ballroom dance?"

"One of my part-time jobs during high school and college. Classes always have more women than men. One of my grandmother's friends owned a dance studio. She hired two of us. Quite coincidentally, the other guy became a doctor, too."

By her eyes, he could tell she'd gone somewhere else in her head again. Curiosity burned within him. This woman intrigued him like no other. Such complex intricacy. So many levels.

"I've always wanted to learn to waltz."

Niko had the strongest urge to hold her in his arms right then and there. But he reached deep and found the gentleman his grandmother had instilled in him. "Dessert first?"

She cast her eyes down. "If you want."

He wanted. But not food. "You're all the dessert I need."

There it was again. The sparkle as Annalise looked around the table at the other guests. "If you'll excuse us."

Niko tried to read the message behind the look the entertainment director gave him. He wasn't sure what exactly the man was trying to say but he had a feeling it had something to do with being very protective of his ship's doctor.

The director needn't worry. Niko would cut off his right hand before he harmed Annalise. He'd never felt like that with any other woman. Why did he feel that way now?

He had to remember that in a few short days anything between them would have to be over.

"Ready?" Annalise looked expectantly at him.

Ready? He wasn't quite sure what he was ready for. He only knew that if she was involved then yes. He was ready for anything.

CHAPTER ELEVEN

"LOOK UP," NIKO whispered in her ear.

Annalise looked up, away from her feet, to drown in those tiger eyes. She missed a step.

"Sorry."

"Don't be sorry. Everybody has to learn." As his breath warmed her ear, raising shivers along her nape, his big hand guided her in the right direction.

The deck was dark enough that the few couples on the makeshift dance floor were nothing but faceless shadows. The band was good—as was all the entertainment the cruise line provided.

The vastness of the night sky fell into the ocean, wrapping them in velvet darkness. Stars came and went overhead as clouds floated by. The moon was a gray crescent sliver overhead. The sea breeze was just enough to make Niko's body next to hers pleasurably warm.

She was acutely aware of his hand on her bare back as the pressure of his palm suggested a backward step.

"One, two, three," he counted for her. "Turn, two, three."

His words were like a litany that went beyond hearing, moving her body beyond her conscious control.

She felt like quicksilver, an extension of the music, part of the night.

"Exquisite," he murmured.

Annalise knew he wasn't talking about her waltz.

She was floating, floating with no concept of space and time. All she knew was Niko's body next to hers, floating, floating in perfect rhythm.

A lovely surreal mist surrounded her reality as she let her essence free.

As the ocean's waves and swells picked up, Niko held her closer, making their steps smaller and smaller until they were barely swaying.

"Look up," he murmured.

She did.

His mouth covered hers and she parted her lips, tasting, inhaling the scent of him, moving closer at the pressure of his hand on her back. She could read it through the energy he surrounded her with. He needed her.

She understood. She needed him. She answered his need, giving, taking, asking, demanding until she lost herself in his kiss.

Her world spun around her as she held onto Niko, secure in his steadiness. Right now, at this moment, he was the center of her universe, directing the moon and the stars. Directing each beat of her heart.

Annalise gasped, realizing she'd forgotten to breathe, realizing the music was now only in her head.

His voice rumbled through her. "Want to continue this in my suite?"

She blinked as if coming out from under hypnosis. The part of her that had ceased to think and could only feel said, "Yes." She sounded dreamy, drugged.

Then panic began to thin out the haze of her fantasy world. Old panic that should have long since been put to bed.

No. She wouldn't let that lovely floating feeling go that easily.

"Yes," she said again, wincing at the way her voice quivered, regretting that she was now anticipating the clamminess that would soon be rising up in her, the way it always did, wishing away a past that kept following her long after her assailant had been locked away.

No, she would not be a prisoner to another man's crime.

Niko placed the gentlest of kisses along her nape. One long finger traced down her spine and his hand splayed across her bare back, supporting her as she leaned away enough to look into his face.

Deliberately, she met his eyes. "Yes."

She sounded firm this time, sure of herself, bold and daring.

Intense desire swept through Niko, making his palms sweat and his heart race. Triumph!

He'd felt her hesitate. Then he'd poured on the charm, following his gut instincts to know what she needed from him, and it had worked.

Annalise. He would soon be running his hands over her, tasting her, feeling her respond—feeling himself respond.

And that's where the apprehension surfaced. Apprehension that this would mean more to her than...

No. That this would mean more to *him* than he was prepared for it to mean.

Logically, he knew he was being unreasonable. They had only met a handful of days ago under circumstances that were totally out of the norm for him. Circumstances that weren't made for anything deep or serious.

Hell, *he* wasn't made for anything deep or serious, no matter what the circumstances.

This was not a time for a game of cat and mouse with a mouse who didn't understand he would be letting her loose as soon as he'd caught her.

That he'd sensed her pulling away was solid proof that this shouldn't be happening like this. Not without the full truth revealed between them.

He was a fool for asking her to join him in his suite. He was a fool for continuing to hold her in his arms when he should be putting distance between them.

Annalise did it for him. Putting her hands on his chest, she pushed him away. "What? I wasn't supposed to agree?"

Niko looked up at the night sky that only seconds before had been comforting in its cocooning darkness.

Now the vastness looked daunting, imposing and desolate.

He looked into her eyes, wanting her to see what he didn't know how to say. "I wasn't supposed to ask."

She darted a quick glance at his ring finger, then back up to his face. "You're not married, are you?"

"No." A raw, self-deprecating laugh worked its

way through his chest. "No, I'm not the marrying kind."

"I don't understand." Tears welled, although
Niko knew she was trying to hold them back. She
was wounded, rejected, hurt. Her pain caused him
misery.

"You're not the kind of woman to love and leave.
You deserve someone who will stay."

Fire erased the tears in her eyes. "Who are you
to say what kind of woman I am?"

"I'm the man who desires you with a want greater
than any need I've ever felt before. But I can't take
the guilt of feeling I might be coercing you into
something you'd regret tomorrow morning."

"Coerce? As in force?" She gave him a wry
smile. "Seduce maybe, but not coerce."

"Seduce then." He rubbed his hand through his
hair. "I'm sorr—"

She held a finger up to his lips, not touching him
by scant millimeters. "No. Don't say it."

He breathed in her lavender lotion, clenching his
fists to keep from pulling her to him and kissing
her until the shreds of his own good sense floated
away on an ocean of pheromones.

Not trusting himself to speak, he gave her a parting nod and turned away.

But she caught his arm. Her hand on his sleeve

held him still better than any pair of handcuffs ever made.

"What would it take—?" She stopped. Licked her lips and swallowed, then continued. "What would it take to convince you that a shipboard romance would be enough for me?"

"In the state I'm in right now? Not much." His mouth quirked up as he said it. Humor instead of hurt. It was what he did.

But then he pressed his lips together tightly and thought, respecting that she'd asked a serious question. "Come to me. No stars. No wine. No music. No romance." Niko knew his conditions would drive her away. She was too practical, too guarded, too astute to fall for a guy like him. "Come to me and tell me you want me. Then I'll know."

He turned his back on her and walked away.

With each step he took away from her, Niko felt he was going in the wrong direction. If he'd known it would be this hard, he would have never set foot on this ship.

Perspective, Christopoulos, he reminded himself. This trip was a slice of fantasy out of real time. Annalise would make a nice memory, maybe even a what-if memory. But she could never be his reality. He knew what was important to him and it couldn't include a cruise-ship doctor he would never see again once he disembarked.

What would it feel like when he walked away for good?

Reality made his head ache.

With a sigh Niko headed towards the neon-lit bar with music loud enough to drive throbbing thoughts from his mind.

Through sheer willpower, he kept putting one foot in front of the other until he ended up in a bar so overly loud, so neon flashy and so anonymous he could finally drop the mask of firm decision he'd donned to keep her safe—to keep them both safe—from foolish passion.

Instead, he dropped his head into his hands, not even looking up when he ordered a double Scotch, neat.

CHAPTER TWELVE

ANNALISE SWAM LAPS in the empty adults-only pool until Brandy, who was working the poolside bar, insisted she would grow a mermaid's tail if she didn't come out soon.

Reluctantly, she admitted that going back and forth without getting anywhere was not making progress, only making her exhausted.

How dared he? She scrubbed the excess water from her body then threw the towel into the pool-side bin.

How dared he see through her bravado to the insecurities lying underneath?

Her legs quivered as she made her way back to her cabin. But her physical exhaustion did nothing to diminish her mental anguish or her sexual frustration.

Her body burned for Niko. For that nebulous release she'd heard about, read about, but had never experienced.

Finally, hours after she had pushed her alarm

clock to the floor to hide the mocking numbers, she fell asleep.

Some time during the night she'd had fevered dreams that had left her soaked in sweat. When had that happened? When she had felt like her body was on fire?

She stripped off the oversized T-shirt and gym shorts she usually slept in, avoiding the mirror as she headed for the shower. But then she stopped herself as she realized her nudity, even in the privacy of her own cabin, made her feel uncomfortable.

Annalise gave herself a stern mental shake. If she wasn't comfortable with her own naked body, how could she be okay with Niko's?

Experimentally, shyly, she ran her hands down her curves.

Unknowingly, he'd dared her to explore her own femininity, to explore her own sexuality, to explore him.

And she *would* explore him, every nook and cranny.

Annalise realized she was standing in front of the mirror, her hands propped on her hips. After too many years of glancing away, she took a good, long look.

"Annalise Walcott, you are a fine-looking woman.

A strong woman. A sexy woman—more than sexy enough for Niko Christopoulos. Now, prove it to yourself.'

Her beeper startled her with a beep as it displayed the texted reminder, 'Talent show practice in thirty minutes.'

She had forgotten. Niko and she were to perform in tonight's talent show.

Annalise grinned. She knew exactly what song they would sing together.

Niko's late night and the predicted rain splattering on his cabin window lulled him into sleeping late. He awoke with a start, panic over needing to check Sophie's blood-sugar level sending his adrenal glands going into overdrive until he discovered that Phoebe had already taken care of the whole routine.

He was definitely off balance.

Headachy from his overindulgences at the neon bar, Niko looked over the lyrics he'd just been handed as he arrived at the theater two hours late to practice for the talent show.

You ain't no saint, I ain't your angel.

He knew the song. The melody was simple, the chords basic. Still, it had lots of room for drama. It was a good choice for a quick performance.

Apparently, Annalise had already come and gone. He would practice with a recording and hope they hit their cues right tonight. Thankfully, this selection had a lot of wiggle room to improvise and recover from mistakes.

After an hour and a half of getting comfortable with the finger progressions on his borrowed guitar and singing his part with a throat that needed a spoonful of honey to ease last night's excesses, he decided to spend a quiet couple of hours in the ship's library, reading and napping.

Before he could reach the literary refuge, his twin nephews found him.

Marcus gave him a speculative stare. "Uncle Niko, we were going to rent a couple of video games to play in the video-game room but the desk person said it wasn't authorized. They said we had to have your permission. What's the deal with that?"

"I'll take care of it."

"Or we could just ask Dad for his credit card."

That's all Niko needed this morning, to have to deal with his sweepstakes deception being discovered.

"Where's your dad?"

"He and Mom are hanging out in the adults-only pool area. Something about a hot tub and remembering their youth." Marcus shuddered. "I don't want to think about it."

"And everyone else?"

"Yiayia has the little kids in the kiddie theater, watching a movie. I think Uncle Theo and Aunt Chloe were going back to bed after breakfast." Marcus shrugged. "That's all I know."

"Which game did you want to rent?"

They told him and he promised to join them in the games room as soon as he had it arranged. Maybe blasting a few brain-sucking aliens and saving the planet was what he needed to clear his head.

Distracting himself in the games room was a good plan. It might have even worked if Annalise hadn't had the same idea.

Who would have known Dr. Annalise Walcott had a yen to be a kickboxer?

She barely gave him a nod as she kicked and punched, making the video version of herself teach a harsh lesson to the thugs and muggers of the unreal gamester underworld.

He wished he could be so focused as alien after alien blasted his video avatar into smithereens. Instead, he couldn't take his attention from Annalise, clad in a sports bra and bicycle shorts, virtually fighting her way through the underbelly of society.

To his nephews' exasperation, he wasn't nearly as successful in demolishing the invading aliens as Annalise was in dispatching society's scumbags. But the activity did make the time go quicker.

By mid-afternoon he realized he hadn't eaten all day. It was a good, if not quite valid excuse for his irritability. In the dining room he scarfed down a quick sandwich and a fruit plate then hurried off to costuming, hoping Annalise hadn't picked something totally ludicrous for him to wear.

A large crowd had been driven into the theater by the rain that was continuing to fall throughout the late afternoon. They had already sat through a half dozen acts of dubious quality and were getting restless.

In her white choir robe and feathery angel wings Annalise waited for her cue. Despite her nerves, she was ready to sing the opening bars.

While she could never have stood in front of a room full of people to deliver a speech, this was different. She was singing someone else's words, being someone else, being someone bold and brave and beautiful.

Niko would be entering from the opposite side of the stage. She could hardly wait to see how he

carried off the costume she'd arranged for him—
or to see his reaction to hers.

When she whipped off her angelic robe, she
would be revealing a side of herself no one had
ever seen. That made her extremely apprehensive.
But she was no longer going to let fear stop her
from going after the life she wanted.

And that life was quite a bit different than the
one she'd been living. This life, this cruise-ship
venue, had nurtured her when she'd needed it most
but now she had grown past that need.

Doctors Without Borders. She'd been thinking
about it for quite a while. She'd been delivering
donated medicines and doing volunteer work for
the poor of the islands whenever the ship dropped
anchor ever since she'd started working for the
cruise line, a practice she'd learned from her pre-
decessor. The charity work had been the most re-
warding part of her trips. After hearing the passion
in Niko's voice when he'd talked about it, she was
ready to make it her full-time work.

Since she would be leaving the ship at the end
of this run, she would leave them with something
to remember her by.

As the captain's personal stewards finished up
their shaky barbershop quartet to politely enthu-

siastic applause, Annalise let out a sigh of relief. They wouldn't be a hard act to follow.

The curtain fell and the production manager gave her a nod along with a thumbs-up.

She hurried out to take her place next to the Styrofoam column that temporarily hid Niko's borrowed guitar. For some reason she'd never doubted he'd be up to the task of pulling off this act. He was the kind of man who inspired confidence.

As the curtain rose, her confidence fell. All those people clapping, waiting, listening for her.

With the floodlights in her eyes, she couldn't make out details, but she saw a movement at the edge of the stage. Niko.

She was not alone in this.

He strode out, tight jeans, black T-shirt and black leather jacket. His tiger eyes gleamed as he ignored the crowd and gave her his full attention.

He stood so close her wings brushed his midnight hair.

"Ready?" He grabbed his microphone from the stand.

She left hers in the stand, clasping her hands angelically instead. "Ready."

As the pianist played the intro lines, Annalise took a deep breath, held it, then belted out the notes right on key.

You say someday the right man will come along,
The man who will see my angel wings and hear my angel song.
But I say to you, you're wrong.
Because that day has already come and gone.
And it looks like you're here to stay.

He leaned in close, so close she see the sparks in his eyes as he glanced her way then focused on the audience.

I may be here today, but I won't stay.
I'm the kind of man that plays then goes away.
You deserve a man who will never stray.

Niko grabbed the guitar and did a screaming instrumental of angry chords before cueing back to the lyrics.

I've got a wandering soul
And I'm not made to grow old
In one place, even if that place is heaven.

This was the moment Annalise had been planning for. As Niko performed the next guitar break, she unzipped the heavy, shapeless robe and wings and let them fall to the floor, stretching her arms wide to revel in the form and freedom of the tiny, shiny gold spandex dress.

Vaguely, Annalise heard the roar of the onlookers, but nothing spoke as loudly to her as the look in Niko's eyes.

If his tiger eyes were anything to go by, he was definitely feeling carnivorous.

She struck a pose, leaning in close and daring to look straight into those mesmerizing eyes as a dangerous thrill energized her like a bolt of lightning.

Plucking her microphone from the stand, she sang.

You ain't no saint. I ain't your angel.
I'm the woman who can match you, play for play.
Day by day.

She grinned, growling the words out.

And night by night.

Niko missed a beat as he swallowed. Then caught up with her.

Night by night
Day by day

You're the woman who can match me
Play by play.
And I'm the man that can match you, too.
Because I love you.

Together they sang,

Because I love you.

Annalise didn't even realize the curtain had fallen until it started to open again. From the dazed look on Niko's face he hadn't realized it either.

Amazingly, he looked away first, a bashful casting down of his eyes.

"Good job," she whispered as they took their bows.

He nodded, still not looking at her. "And you."

She grabbed his hand and almost dropped it again as heat travelled up her arm and throughout her body. Remembering who she wanted to be, she clasped it tighter as they took another bow and then she led him offstage.

Once alone backstage, he turned to her, searching her face. "Wow."

"Wow back at you."

And then the Christopoulos family interrupted, whooping and laughing and complimenting them.

How could she resent the intrusion when it was all too easy to breathe in the love, the cherishing and solidarity they gave Niko and, by extension, her, too?

What would it be like to be part of a family like this?

But they would expect more than she could give.

Niko lifted her chin. "What's wrong?"

"I need to change before these shoes start to pinch."

He eyed the high-heeled sexy shoes that made her legs look miles long. "That's a shame."

"Life's not fair." She shrugged, trying to smile through the truth. But the twisted feel of her lips told her she had failed.

When one of the twins said he was hungry, Annalise checked the clock. The show had run overtime and it was time for supper. Niko's brother Stephen nodded toward Sophie and said, "My turn," as the family gravitated toward the door.

Annalise knew that supper would be filled with joyous noise, kudos for Niko and endless toasts offered with unconditional love.

Niko called back to them, "Don't wait for me."

Annalise would not be the one to keep him from his family. "No, Niko. Go with them. I may join you later."

Sophie crossed her arms and planted her feet. "I want Uncle Niko to give me my shot. You hurt, Uncle Stephen."

Stephen sent Niko an apologetic look. "Maybe you can show me again."

Niko looked at Annalise as if he were seeking her permission. She nodded, releasing him.

"Sure, brother." He reached down and took Sophie's hand. "Let's show Uncle Stephen how brave girls do this, okay?"

Annalise watched the Christopoulos family troop out, looking and sounding so much like each other that anyone would know they were family. What would it be like to look into a child's face and see your own reflected there?

She could usually stave off her utter aloneness, the lack of a legacy to prove she'd left her mark on the world.

But today her future was harder to accept. One hand drifted to her damaged womb, which could never carry a child, and the other hand covered her damaged heart, which could never carry the love of a man.

She waited for the anger to well up within her, to burn through the melancholy that always followed her reminder of reality. Waited to feel the remembered fear when her mother's boyfriend had loomed over her and she had shut her eyes tight no matter how loudly he'd shouted at her to open them.

She took a breath. Anger and fear and despair were ugly scars she didn't have to wear.

Instead, she thought about Niko. About being held in his arms as they swayed to the music under the stars. About feeling admired and respected whenever he looked at her. About how she would let her passion build and grow when they made love.

And they would make love.

She hung up the leather jacket Niko had worn. It was the only thing he'd needed from the costume wardrobe. The rest of the outfit had been all his.

With measured steps she trod onto the curtained stage.

Carefully, in the tight dress and high heels that she was so unaccustomed to, she stooped to pick up the heavy robe and angel wings from where they had fallen.

She'd tried to have a relationship before with her medical school study partner. They had become great platonic friends, with an easy way between them. When she'd asked, pleaded, for his help, he had agreed.

They'd both tried to make it work—she'd wanted

it to work so badly. She'd wanted to prove to herself that her rapist wouldn't win in the end. He'd been kind, gentle and mercifully quick.

But all she'd managed had been distant numbness. Would it be the same with Niko? Would that fire in his touch, that tingling warmth that penetrated her thickest barriers, flame out when it reached her icy core?

Or would he be the one to unthaw her, heart and soul? She could walk away now. Never know. Never fail. Always think it might have worked out, while sanctimoniously congratulating herself on following the rules.

No shipboard romance. No knowing to what heights and depths this chemistry between them could take her. No having to say goodbye when this trip came to its end.

No guts, no glory.

Now was the time. Niko was the man. Tonight she would learn what it was to glory in being a woman, body and soul.

CHAPTER THIRTEEN

NIKO STOOD ON his veranda, his hands gripping the rail as he looked out onto the starlit ocean going past. He'd thought about spending another evening at the bar but muddling his thinking by drinking too many glasses of forgetful juice wouldn't solve his problem. Neither would going up to the top deck.

Would she come to him? So much depended on it.

He'd had it all mapped out, even to the point of accepting that his family wouldn't be happy with his decisions. He'd been so sure of what he wanted. But now…

Now he wanted more than he could have.

What if he loved her?

He shook his head. There was no *what-if*.

He couldn't imagine getting off this ship and never seeing her again.

What was he going to do?

Annalise knocked. Once. Sharply. Then turned away to flee back to the safety of her own berth.

The door opened and Niko reached out, catching her hand and pulling her to him. He bent his lips to her ear. "Annalise. You came." He breathed it like she was an answer to his prayers.

She inhaled his scent, wanting to hold it deep within her forever.

"About your rules, Niko. No stars. No wine. No music. No romance." She paused. "I've decided you don't get to make all the rules."

She set an ice-filled wine bucket on the counter then went to the wall of windows, looking out at the night sky where the last of the rainclouds were skittering away, exposing a handful of twinkling stars. "What's sex without romance?"

As he walked up behind her, she willed herself to stay relaxed.

Still, he noticed. "Problem?"

What should she tell him? "I don't usually…"

He moved a footstep away. "This isn't your first time, is it?"

Her laugh was much too harsh, much too revealing. "My previous experiences haven't been that great."

"Want to tell me about it?"

"Maybe another time." She closed her eyes. "Tonight I want something more than talk."

"Are you sure you want to do this?" He took another step away. "With me?"

"Yes." She didn't dare turn around, afraid she might show him something with her eyes that she would rather keep to herself.

He was silent for so long that a dozen stars had time to make their appearance. Annalise raised her palm to the glass, anchoring herself.

Ever so lightly, he rested his fingers on the nape of her neck.

She couldn't stop her instinct to hunch her shoulders and shrink away.

He dropped his hand.

"I can't—we can't do this with you being frightened." He backed away, sitting on the bed. "Annalise, you need to tell me what is scaring you."

For the longest time Annalise stood as still as a statue, staring out at the stars. Finally, she sighed deeply, looked at him, avoiding his eyes, then looked at the door.

Just when Niko thought she would go, she sat down next to him, her thigh touching his.

In the dark, in the silence, Annalise said, "I was sixteen when I was raped by my mother's boyfriend. I was afraid to tell her. Afraid she'd say it was my fault. Afraid she'd kick me out of our apartment. That happened to a girl who lived down the hall from us. She didn't even make it a week on the streets before they found her body. I figured one rape was better than a gang rape."

Niko felt such rage race through him he had to use all his concentration to keep his hand from squeezing hers.

"He got me pregnant. I tried to hide it from her but she figured it out when I was sick every morning for two weeks. She took me to this place above a bar and a stinky, greasy woman…she did things to me and I bled."

Bile rose in Niko's throat. He couldn't imagine what the sixteen-year-old Annalise had overcome. Few people, especially teens, would have had the mental strength. She had not only survived but thrived.

"She said the bleeding would stop after a while, but it didn't. Finally, my mother drove me to the hospital and dropped me off at the emergency-room door. She didn't come back for me."

Annalise was squeezing his hand so tightly his fingers tingled.

Niko had to swallow hard to ask, "Afterwards, where did you go?"

"At first I was in a home for wayward teens, repeat offenders in trouble with the law—not that I

was one. It was the only place they had to put me."
Her laugh was like sandpaper. "And I'd thought I
was pretty tough."

"Then what happened?"

"The social worker from the hospital kept looking for a better place for me. She finally got a
church-sponsored boarding school with an attached private high school to take me in. I was
one of their charity cases. It wasn't bad and the
education I received was outstanding. I was able
to earn scholarships that paid for a lot of my college and medical-school expenses."

"Annalise, I don't know what to say." Niko
wanted to hold her and protect her from all the
bad things in life. But he was too late.

She brushed the tears from his face that he hadn't
realized he'd shed.

"Hold me, Niko. Keep me safe tonight."

Could he do this?

His throat closed so that he could only nod. For
the first time in his life he understood the healing
power of being there. A gentle touch was all the
action desired or required.

Annalise curled up in his bed and he curled up
around her, cocooning her.

And they slept.

In the morning, she was gone.

* * *

Annalise hurried down the gangway, pulling her cart of donated medicines behind her. The island's refugee camp would be anxiously awaiting her delivery of supplies as well as her skills as a physician. Her charity work was one of the reasons she loved her job so much.

That's why, when she'd dropped her application for Doctors Without Borders in the outgoing mail packet early that morning, she'd been certain she'd made the right career-change decision.

She hurried, very aware that the camp would have been expecting her much earlier.

They'd docked sometime during the night and she'd planned to be off the ship at daybreak, but she'd overslept. She was certain she'd never slept so deeply in her life as when she'd been wrapped in Niko's arms.

If only every night's sleep could be as restful.

A wave of sadness threatened to swamp her but Annalise refused to dwell on what couldn't be.

A shipboard relationship, by its nature, was impermanent. With Niko, there were no expectations and no disappointments. She would just be sure to make the most of the little time they had left together.

Niko Christopoulos would always have a special

place in her healing heart. Because of him there was a profound difference very deep down within her, like cleansing light had been shone into the dark corners of her psyche.

But it was better that way. Even if Niko was an adventurer now, she'd seen how much he loved his nieces and nephews and how much he admired his sisters-in-law. He would want a family of his own someday. And that was something she could never give him. The thought of being separated from him made her feet feel heavy.

"Annalise, wait up." Niko's deep voice startled her from her thoughts.

She slowed her pace and looked behind her to see him trotting toward her, concern on his face.

"Niko, what's wrong?"

"What's wrong?" He rubbed his hand across his eyes. "I woke up and found you gone. That's what's wrong."

She grinned, both relieved and flattered. "Not everyone is on vacation, Niko Christopoulos."

"You're working?"

"Volunteer work. This island has several refugee camps. People try to navigate the Mediterranean Sea and this is as far as they get sometimes. Different charity organizations have set up clinics. I do what I can when we come through this way."

She started pulling the cart toward shore again, carefully concentrating to keep it from rolling out of control.

"I'll go with you."

"What about your family?"

"We've all had quite a bit of togetherness lately. I think we're ready to have some apart time." He commandeered the cart from her, easily keeping the pace steady.

"But you'll miss the tourist attractions."

"What I miss is practicing medicine. I'm not made to be idle this long."

"I understand. The few times I've tried to give myself a break from seeing patients between cruises, I've wound up being irritated with the world and itching to go back to my work. Being a doctor isn't just what I do, it's who I am."

Niko flashed her a brilliant smile. "You do understand."

"This one is not as advanced as some of the other free clinics on the Caribbean islands where we call," she warned him. "But working with Doctors Without Borders, you're used to a lot worse conditions, I'll bet."

"I've seen some primitive environments," he agreed.

Annalise thought about mentioning her recent

decision and asking if he would mind if she requested to be assigned with him but now she was thinking that might be a bit presumptuous. If Niko could get tired of his awesome family, what would he think of being saddled with her, a virtual stranger?

Only Niko didn't feel like a stranger. He felt like someone she'd been waiting to meet her whole life.

Which meant that if they were assigned together, the arrangement could get complicated.

She should probably let fate take care of that little issue.

As Niko dragged the cart through the streets, past the brightly colored tourist shops and the clapboard houses with their white-picket-fenced yards, he asked, "What am I hauling?"

"Supplies. Donations from different charity groups. We have a nice collection of used eyeglasses. So many children and adults can't learn to read because they don't see well enough to make out the letters. The glasses are always a welcome donation."

Niko nodded. "Glasses are one of the sought-out donations on missions I've been a part of, too."

They weaved in and out of streets and alleys. The paint on the buildings became older and sparser until there were no buildings at all. A tent city sat on a span of vacant lots in front of them. Little more than a few strands of sparse weedy grass separated the tarps and quilts and stitched-together rags from each other.

For some, the hodgepodge temporary living quarters didn't appear to be so temporary but rather looked like journey's end. People of all ages sat outside their tents or walked aimlessly from place to place.

Annalise led the way toward the center of the encampment, where four sturdy canvas tents stood with their side walls rolled up.

"That one." She pointed to the tent on the far left.

And that's when they got busy. For the rest of the day, far into the late afternoon, Annalise and Niko saw patient after patient.

As Niko carefully lanced an eardrum, fluid-filled almost to bursting, on a toddler, Annalise said her goodbyes to the staff. Most she had never met before as they changed so frequently. But a few she had known for quite a while. She explained that she wouldn't be back, but her new physician's assistant would come next trip if possible.

The staff took her departure in their stride. They had never known consistency. They just did the best they could with what they had.

As soon as Niko was done, she pointed to her

watch. "We've got to get back to the ship. It's getting dark."

They walked in silence for the most part. Leaving behind such squalor for the luxury of the cruise liner, it always took Annalise a moment to adjust.

At the bottom of the gangway, Niko stopped.

"You were great today."

"You, too."

"Especially with the children. You'll make a great mother, Annalise."

No. She wouldn't. She couldn't. The botched abortion had taken away any possibility of her bearing children. "Not in the plan." It came out flippantly to hide her sorrow.

Niko gave her a long look. "I owe you an apology. I underestimated you."

"Most people do." Annalise shrugged it off then blatantly inspected Niko. "Good looks, expensive watch, attitude of nonchalance. I'll bet most people underestimate you, too."

"A man can be more than one thing."

"Like a good lover as well as a good doctor?"

He stopped walking. "What are you saying, Annalise?"

"I'd like to try it again." She licked her bottom lip. "If you're willing."

"With you, I'm always willing." The words were right but the tone was hesitant.

She put her hand on his arm. "Niko, please. Don't. Don't treat me like I'm fragile. I don't break."

"Tell me what you want, Annalise."

"I want to feel like a real woman, a woman who can make a man's blood run hot. I want you to make love to me because you think I'm sexy, not because you feel sorry for me."

"You trust me, don't you, Annalise?"

"I do trust you, Niko."

"Then believe me when I say I don't do pity sex."

"I'm trying."

"What can I do to prove it to you?"

"Make love to me like I was any other woman."

"Oh, no, Annalise. I can't do that. You're not any other woman."

"Because I'm different."

"Because you're special."

Outside his cabin door, he asked her once more. "Are you sure?"

"Yes, Niko, I want to make love to you more than I've ever wanted anything in my whole life."

He opened the door for her and followed her in. Very quietly, he whispered in her ear, "Let's make this the first-time experience it should have been."

Annalise swallowed past the lump in her throat. "I would like that."

Slowly, gently, he reached up and touched her hair. She breathed in the scent of him as he ran his fingertips across her shoulders. Then he glided his fingers along the edge of her bra, barely brushing the side of her breast.

"Yes?" he asked, his voice throaty, needy, full of want for her.

"Yes." She turned in his arms, putting them chest to chest.

His hand traced her back through her thin T-shirt, leaving a trail of flame sizzling down her spine.

She lifted her mouth, needing to taste him. He met her lips with his own, teasing her mouth until she opened for him. Her knees weakened as the world around her began to blur, soft and hazy and out of focus. Niko was all that mattered.

His big hands brushed over her shoulders and down her arms, capturing her. A distant part of her mind waited for the flinch that would bring disappointment to his eyes. That's when the numbness would begin.

But she didn't flinch, didn't step back, didn't

squeeze her eyes closed. Instead, her body leaned in as her instincts trusted Niko to bear her weight.

He carried her to the bed, gracefully sitting her in his lap as he leaned against the headboard.

"Niko." She said his name, soft and husky with an underlying plea for more.

"I'm yours for the taking." He'd heard her and was willing to give her what she needed. He spread his arms wide, giving her total access.

The moonlight through the open window gave the room a feeling of a black and white movie. He made a hell of a leading man.

The look of desire in his eyes emboldened her so she felt like his femme fatale.

Starting with his top button, her clumsy fingers pushed it free of the buttonhole. With her index finger she traced inside the open V. Under her fingertip his chest hair felt coarse while his skin was smooth.

He groaned, deep and long and soulful. "What sweet agony from my exquisite Annalise."

"Should I go faster?"

"No. Please." He kissed the tips of her fingers. "I want this to last forever."

She worked the next button free but couldn't stop herself from going for the next and the one after that until his shirt lay open, exposing his chest and abs. She splayed her hands across his chest, feeling the twin peaks of his flat pecs respond to her touch. Experimentally, she rubbed them. He sucked in his breath like he'd been sucker punched.

She'd done that. She'd taken his breath away. A feeling of power rolled through her.

"Are you okay?" She couldn't keep the provocative pride from her voice when she asked any more than she could keep herself from flicking those sensitive peaks again.

"Vixen." The amusement in his voice caressed her while goading her to continue.

But her own body ached for his exploring touch.

"Tell me, Annalise. Tell me what you want."

"Take my top off." That had sounded demanding, hadn't it? "Please," she added.

"Absolutely." He reached for the hook at the nape of her neck. He pulled her T-shirt over her head.

The appreciated groan he gave her made the heat rise deep down inside that place that had never felt warm before.

She revelled in the way his eyes went dark when she reached back to unhook her bra.

So much appreciation. So much awe. So much desire.

Bare to the night air, her nipples peaked, aching for his attention. "Kiss me."

Obediently, he reverently suckled first one taut tip, then the other. The moan that escaped sounded like it came from the depths of her.

"Thank you." She sounded wispy, breathless.

"My pleasure." His voice was a deeply sincere growl.

"The panties match. Want to see?"

"Yes, oh, please, yes."

Smiling, she shimmied out of her shorts, revealing her newest purchase. No granny panties for her tonight.

In the gray moonlight, her black panties contrasted with the paleness of her skin, making her feel naughty and so very sexy.

She pushed Niko backwards until his knees hit the back of her bed. Fluidly, he lay back on the bed and she climbed on top of him.

Under her, Niko grimaced and shifted his weight.

Immediately, she lifted herself so she straddled him without holding him down. "Your leg?"

He grinned up at her. "No."

"Then what?"

"These jeans are getting a bit tight."

"Oh." Her own naïveté made her blush.

"Do you think you might want to take them off soon? Or at least unzip them?" Her hand hovered over the zipper as the intimacy of what she was about to do made her hesitate.

He grinned at her, his dimples deep as a cloud shifted and a moonbeam splashed across his face. "Please?"

Shyness won out. "You do it."

"Cover my hand." He waited until her hand rested on his before he unbuttoned and unzipped.

"Better?" she asked, even though she could see his jeans restricted him.

"Not quite." He lifted his hips, putting his rough jeans in contact with the sensitive ache that only the thin silk of her panties protected.

Beneath her, he pushed his jeans off his hips and thighs then kicked them free, all the while bucking underneath her, making her want… Oh, how she wanted.

She marveled at the throbbing that needed fulfillment. She had been sure such passion was only a myth made up for movies and books.

Niko drew in a deep breath. "You are so beautiful."

She stilled, realizing what a silhouette they made in the moonlight.

Quickly, she pushed down her panties. Just as quickly, Niko grabbed protection from the nightstand. His tip nudged her bud and she guided him inside her. They fit together as if they were made for each other. And somewhere in the joyous center of her soul she knew they had been.

She rode him, with her back arched and her hands braced against his chest. His lean body under hers responded to her pace and rhythm, faster and faster until they were both gasping for breath.

A throaty, wordless note of ecstasy came from her throat. Niko answered with his own deep roar of celebration. Together they pulsed in time with the universe.

After an eternity of bliss Annalise lay spent on Niko's chest as he brushed his hand along her back.

"Annalise?"

"Hmm?"

"Tomorrow morning we make port in Malaga. Whatever you have planned, I want to be part of it."

"No plans for Malaga." Annalise thought hard about what she was about to offer. Would it be more painful to experience what being a part of a family was like or more lonely to forgo the whole experience?

Better to have loved and lost than never to have loved at all. Poets were supposed to be experts at this sort of thing, weren't they?

"I've got the perfect idea for your whole family. Do you think—?"

"I think I want you all to myself."

"This is supposed to be your family vacation."

He grinned at her. "Now you sound like one of the Christopoulos women."

"If only you could be so lucky." Too late, Annalise realized what she'd implied.

Niko lost his grin. "If only…"

He said it low, but Annalise was too tuned in to his every breath to have missed it.

Only what would she do with it?

"Your idea?" Niko prompted.

"Malaga has some great bike tours. They even rent bikes with carriages on the back for Yiayia and the little ones. There's one tour in particular I've heard great things about that I think your family will enjoy."

Looking deceptively like a tame house cat, Niko turned those tiger eyes on her. But she'd seen them blaze with hunger only a short time earlier and was not deceived. "I'm sure my family will enjoy it, but what's in it for me and you?"

"I don't know about you, Niko Christopoulos, but I would love to spend a day with your family." Had Niko heard her yearning to experience being a part of a family underneath her light and breezy tone? She turned away in case her expression gave her away.

Niko came up behind her, giving her the lightest of kisses along her nape. "My family will love spending the day with you as well." Those kisses deepened as they travelled across her throat and down her breasts.

"How about room service tonight?"

"Your family—"

"Will have me all day tomorrow. Tonight I'm yours." He stopped kissing her a lip's width from the tip of her breast. "If you want me."

His breath on her sensitive skin made her ache so deeply she groaned her answer.

And Annalise found new pleasures she would never have imagined on her own. Much, much later, as she lay in his arms while he slept, she thought about all she had learned from Niko. The stuff that dreams are made of...

But who could go back to living on dreams of the heavens when she'd touched those glorious heights themselves?

Some time in the wee hours of the morning Niko felt Annalise shift, tidying up the bedcovers as if she were tidying up their relationship.

"Annalise?"

She laced her fingers through his. "The way you

say my name makes me feel like the most special woman on earth."

"Then you've caught my meaning exactly right."

"Tell me what to do to make you feel special, too."

Niko had never felt so honored. "That you want me to feel that way does the trick for me."

She unlaced her fingers and sat up, letting the sheets fall to her waist. Moonlight showed her beautiful breasts full and perfect for his hands. He gave in to desire and reached toward her, cupping one, savoring the weight in his palm.

"So beautiful."

She reached up and brushed his hair from his eyes. "So are you."

"Tell me what you want, Annalise. Tell me what I can give to you."

"I want you," she said, shifting under him. "I want to feel your touch on every inch of me. I want to be so feverish with needing to feel you in me that I scream with desire."

"Should I start here?" Niko traced her ear then nibbled on the sensitive rim. "And should I taste you as well?"

"Y-e-s." She drew the word out, like she never wanted to let it go.

"And then move to here?" He trailed kisses down

her neck, smiling when she grabbed his shoulders and pulled him closer.

"Now. I want you now." She wrapped her legs around him to pull him closer still.

As a gentleman, Niko complied.

And when they came together, each shouting the other's name, Niko had never had a more special moment in his life.

CHAPTER FOURTEEN

ANNALISE HAD BEEN to Malaga many times before, but seeing it through Niko's eyes made all the difference. When she'd recommended the tapas and wine bike tour for the family, they had insisted she come too.

For the first time in her life Annalise felt like she could understand the enormity of being accepted. Along with the whole Christopoulos clan, Annalise cycled along the tapas and wine tour route, eating, drinking and laughing. The younger nieces and nephews took turns riding with Yiayia in a carriage behind a bicycle, which the two older nephews were coerced into manning, while all the Christopoulos men opted for bicycles built for two with their women.

No one blinked an eyelash when Annalise paired up with Niko although she did catch a few winks behind her back.

It was a tour after the Christopoulos family's heart.

At their first stop Stephen raised his glass in a toast to Annalise, with great thanks for the suggestion of the bike tour. When Annalise followed it up with a toast to the strong backs and legs of the Christopoulos twins, the hardy laughs and cheers made her felt like one of their own.

Soon she was stuffed with olives and cheese and fried squid and was giddy from a bit more vino dulce than she was accustomed to drinking.

"This looks interesting. Want to try it?" She held a tapas up to Niko to taste.

He nibbled it from her fingers. "Mmm."

Stephen leaned forward and watched him chew.

"He swallowed it." Stephen high-fived his wife. "Annalise, you are some special lady."

Phoebe explained. "Niko is our picky eater. He won't put anything in his mouth without knowing exactly what it is first."

Niko smiled. "I'll eat anything from the hands of a goddess."

At every stop Yiayia charmed the chefs into giving her inside information, showing such appreciation for their skills that they were bringing the family their specialties to taste.

Cooking meant so much to them, especially to Yiayia and Stephen. It was a part of who they were even more than what they did.

Like medicine was to Niko and to Annalise.

Annalise rubbed her full stomach. The tapas bars of Malaga would not soon forget the Christopoulos family.

Annalise understood. A Christopoulos was not an easy person to forget. She was certain that, no matter what happened, she would remember Niko throughout eternity.

By the time they all reached their last stop, the beach at the fishing village of El Palo, the children were happy to build sandcastles while the adults and teens rested and watched.

The Christopoulos men procured beach towels and spread them on the sand, each trying to be more gallant than the others as they extended a helping hand to their women.

Annalise couldn't help pretending she was a part of this great loving family. She was so full of food and wine she could be excused for letting the line between fantasy and reality blur a bit, couldn't she?

Sitting on the beach, leaning back against Niko, Annalise had never felt more content.

Niko leaned forward and whispered in her ear, "I think this is the happiest day I have ever lived."

While he didn't say it, Annalise took liberties in thinking that his happiness was in some small part because she was there.

She knew he was the source of *her* bliss.

"Me, too," she said.

Her voice did things to him deep down that he would never have imagined were possible. His heart beat faster, his breathing deepened, and his hands itched to run along her arms and feel her silky-smooth skin.

He gave a quick look around to see if they had an audience, but his brothers were giving all their attention to their wives while Yiayia and the twins watched the little ones.

As shy as Annalise was in public, he took a chance and dropped a kiss on her neck simply because he couldn't help himself. Annalise leaned her head, giving him better access to drop a second one on top of the first.

Apparently he wasn't quick enough because Marcus gave him a thumbs-up. Thankfully, Annalise didn't notice or if she did, she no longer cared that his family saw their public displays of affection.

He was hoping it was the latter. All day he'd fought the urge to kiss her in front of strangers, which only made his anticipation of their time alone tonight much more intense.

He would have stayed there forever if not for

the children becoming too cold and wet from the spray of the ocean.

Reluctantly they headed back to the ship. The only thought that made leaving the beach bearable was the thought of Annalise in his bed.

His anticipation was rewarded.

Still shy with him, she asked permission to touch him here and there. Knowing what she was about to do then feeling her gentle, hesitant exploration touched him in ways beyond the physical.

Lying with his hands laced behind his head, he encouraged Annalise to explore. Whatever made her happy made him ecstatic.

She coasted her hands and then her mouth over him, eliciting the most wonderful pleasure he had ever known.

While the night started out for her benefit, her tender explorations quickly turned the tables, making it the most memorable night he'd ever had.

He had a strong feeling that each night with Annalise would be more memorable than the last.

As he was about to grasp a bigger concept, Annalise straddled him. Any logical thought patterns he'd been about to form completely fled his brain while a more primeval part of his body took over.

Softly, sweetly, she mounted him and they came

together, swirling, swirling in a haze so rich with the rhythm of love Niko felt her whole body throb in tune with his.

As she lay collapsed on him, he ran his finger down her backside, loving the femininity of her curves.

Annalise soaked up the attention Niko gave her. She'd never had a man want to please her before. All too easily she could become accustomed to feeling cherished. Was it real? Or was it the Christopoulos charm Niko showed all his women?

Happiest day of my life, he'd said. She wanted to believe him. It had certainly been true for her.

But, then, the truth didn't matter, did it? This chance crossing of paths would soon come to an end.

Annalise thought of the enquiry she'd sent to the board of Doctors Without Borders. Maybe, if fate was kind, she and Niko would cross paths again. But Annalise couldn't count on fate.

It was time to practice some self-preservation, time to pull away before Niko left.

On the bedside table Annalise's watch beeped a warning.

Reality. Annalise reached over and checked the time. "I've got to go."

"Go?"

"I've got to dine at the captain's table tonight."

Naked, he stood behind her and turned her to the mirror. He ran his hands over her shoulders. "What can I say…" he gave her a sultry look "…or do to convince you not to go?"

What could he say? *I love you* would work. But he'd given no indication of that.

Lust. Tenderness. Gallantry. Niko had given her all that in spades. But love? There was a good reason for the rule against shipboard romances.

"Say no to the captain. Tell him you have plans with me." He flashed her his best practiced smile.

"Don't do that."

"Don't do what?"

"Don't get all plastic playboy on me because I can't stay and play. Respect me more than that." She had put in too many years of loyal service to want to leave on a bad note. And she needed a clean recommendation.

Plus—and it was a big plus—Niko had taught her to expect respect. Before she'd met him, before she'd seen how much he and his brothers respected all women, including her, she wouldn't have demanded it.

Niko blinked, as if he had been caught looking through her instead of at her. He backed off, leaving her to face the mirror alone. "Sorry.

I've started thinking I have you all to myself. Forgive me?"

She turned to look at him, to read his expression. His face was like an open book. No smooth artifice. No practiced smile. Simply sincerity.

He could put more emotion into those tiger eyes of his than anyone she'd ever met. And she had to admit, his possessiveness *was* on the flattering side.

"Forgiven."

"Thanks." He dropped a chaste kiss on her head that left her wishing for more despite her resolve to put distance between them.

"Tomorrow in port?"

She shook her head. "It's my P.A.'s turn for shore leave. I've got to stay on board and handle the medical suite."

He blew out a breath, looking like a little boy who'd dropped his popsicle in the dirt. "Is it something I did?"

"I'm not on vacation, remember?"

"We're having a private birthday party for Yiayia tomorrow evening. I want you to come." His eyes sharpened, daring her to say no.

Annalise felt honored to be invited but, "It's for family. I don't want to intrude."

"Are you kidding? My family loves you." He

looked into the mirror to shave off his five o'clock shadow. Annalise had suspected that with those dark looks he was a twice a day man.

He kept his attention focused on her reflection as she watched his. Seeing those eyes in the mirror gave her no reprieve.

She swallowed, determined to treat this lightly. "You've got a great family. Everyone meshes so well together, brothers and sisters-in-law and all the children."

He lifted his chin to shave but still didn't break eye contact as if he wanted to judge her reaction. "They're a handful. Especially the nieces and nephews. But being the favorite uncle is the perfect deal. I get to cuddle and spoil them when I'm around, then leave them to their parents when one of us gets cranky."

Annalise had resigned herself to never having babies of her own, but being around the Christopoulos children made her wonder what her life might have been like if she could have been stronger and said no when her mother had marched her up to that filthy back room above the stripper bar and ordered the greasy haired woman there to "get rid of it". But at sixteen, with no means of support and her mother threatening to throw her out of her home, she'd been better at hysterical crying than rational action.

When she saw herself in the mirror, she looked incredibly sad. "They'll expect you to have babies one day."

"They have great expectations." Niko broke eye contact, looking at himself instead of her. That same expression he'd had the first day they'd met, the day he'd called himself the black sheep of the family, resurfaced. "They are destined to be disappointed."

"When you tell them about Doctors Without Borders? How can they be?" She reached out to touch him then dropped her hand as if the barriers going up around him were razor sharp. "Niko, you're a hero. A man to be proud of. The work you do is so important to so many."

She thought about telling him how he inspired her and that she was sending in her own application, but this moment wasn't about her.

He pulled a pair of linen pants from his closet. "The price of these pants would feed a family of five for several months in some of the places I've been."

Annalise waited, knowing there was more.

"Sadly, improving lives isn't all about money. There's a lot of generous people out there. If all it took was throwing money at the problem, poverty would have been stamped out a long time ago. Education, health and developing strong leadership skills in the right people is the answer."

"And that takes time." Wrapped in a towel, Annalise inspected her clothes, wincing at the dirt and sweat from a day of bicycling.

He nodded. His time, his skills, his determination to make a difference were the most valuable contributions he had to give. "The cycle of poverty is so entrenched it all seems hopeless sometimes."

"I've read that burnout among the health-care specialists is a big problem."

He'd seen those who had given their all. War and disease took their toll on the workers, but burnout was a huge hazard, too. That's why trips like this were so important.

"Yes. Burnout is a big deal. I've given a lot of thought on how to deal with it. Vacations like this help."

He needed to remember the joys in life so he could deal with the tragedies. And right now one of those joys was joining his family, listening to the prattle of the little ones, seeing the hope for the future in his older nephews' eyes and knowing that love held the universe together as he watched his brothers and their wives make the world a better place just by being their happy selves and raising their happy families.

What didn't work for him was having a wife and kids at home who waited for the infrequent visits of a husband and father too involved in his work to give enough attention to his family.

Which was why there could never be anything between Annalise and himself beyond what they had now.

"What's wrong? Are you in pain?" Annalise scanned him, making him wish he was still naked. Making him wish for things he could never have, for the woman he could never have.

"I'm fine."

"You groaned and pushed your fist into your stomach."

He used his distracting smile. "It must have been that green stuff you made me eat."

Annalise narrowed her eyes. "If you don't want to tell me what's wrong, that's your business." Then her face went blank. "You're entitled to your privacy."

After being so intimate, the concept of keeping anything from each other seemed to make a mockery of their time together.

But how could he tell her his gut clenched at the idea of leaving her when he left the ship?

Niko turned away to give himself a moment.

Where he had been, what he had done, he had learned to live with loss, only it had never been so personal. And personal made the pain of loss excruciating.

He took another shaky breath, careful to keep his face hidden from Annalise. She could read him like no other.

When he had gathered his composure, he dug through his clothes and handed her one of his T-shirts and a pair of gym shorts. The T-shirt fit her like a dress. The shorts bunched around her waist when she tightened the drawstring enough to keep them from falling off her hips.

"You like?" She held out her hands and turned to model.

Niko caught his breath as he saw the hint of unfettered breasts under the shirt. The woman was breathtaking. "I like—and it has nothing to do with the unique style."

Her laugh brightened his world better than sunshine. "They'll get me back to my room."

"See you at the party tomorrow night?" He saw the hesitation in her eyes. "Please?"

She reached up and ran a finger over his lips. "Has anyone ever said *no to you*?"

"I've heard *no* on occasion and survived. But from you, it would be devastating."

"What would you say if I said the same thing to you?"

"Please, Annalise. It will be our last night on the ship." The implication laid heavy between them.

What could he do? What could he say? The reality of the moment ripped into him. "We can't leave it like this between us."

"Like this?"

"Unfinished." He refused to meet her eyes, afraid of what he might read in them. Which would hurt worse? Resignation or loss?

She nodded. "Closure is a good thing."

No. Closure meant the end. Inside, he screamed it, but he couldn't seem to say it. "Annalise…"

She reached up and cupped his cheek. "I won't go without saying goodbye."

She slipped away before he could answer.

CHAPTER FIFTEEN

ONCE THE DOOR closed behind her, Annalise had to run before all the pent-up emotion made her explode. With tears streaming down her face, she ran down the stairs to her floor. It wasn't that she didn't care who might see her, it was that she couldn't help herself. Running was the only way to keep the pain from overwhelming her. So she ran until her side ached and her lungs burned, her vision so blurry she could barely see.

But, no matter how fast she ran, she couldn't outrun the pain of knowing this had to end.

Then she had to stop. Standing before the door of her room, Annalise had to stop and face herself. Like too many times before, she had nowhere else to go.

She hugged herself, feeling Niko's encompassing shirt around her, smelling his scent rise from her own warm body. Remembering the depth of his eyes when he'd looked at her.

She'd been running away from looking inside herself ever since she'd knocked on Niko's door the first time. But now she'd run into a dead end and the nights spent together had caught up with her.

She had thought making love to Niko would change her inside. And it had, but not the way she had expected.

She had expected to feel braver, more secure, free from her past. Instead, she felt invisible ties binding her to Niko—a man who lived his life without boundaries. What did ties mean to him? She only had to look at his brothers to know.

While she couldn't have children, maybe she could try to be a mother, for Niko's sake?

But what kind of a mother would she be when she really didn't want to be one? The kind of mother *her* mother was, she was afraid.

As much as she wanted it to work, she couldn't be the little woman, barefoot and pregnant, waiting for her man to return.

She couldn't be the woman for him. She couldn't give him what he needed. Family, children, stability to anchor him between missions, to refresh him and send him out again.

Annalise couldn't be that stability for him. Her restlessness was the equal of his. She had her own limits to push. As much as she wanted to be, she was not the home-and-hearth kind.

Niko, with his big heart, would forgo his own

needs and accept what she could give, trying to make it work.

But she would know that she couldn't give him what he needed. Niko would always have a place in his heart for children to carry on his legacy, a hole only his perfect partner could fill. With her, that place would always be empty. She could never do that to the man she loved.

Tomorrow they would dock in Barcelona. While half the passengers would disembark then, the other half, including the Christopoulos family, would continue their trip for another week, touring the Greek isles before flying back home.

For the reduced passenger list, the cruise line didn't need both her and the P.A., though the captain and the cruise line had offered to let her stay on for the extra week without duties as a bonus for her long service. She had thought about staying, but now...

Now she thought about going. She had no future with Niko. More time together would only make leaving harder.

The only thing she knew for sure was that she would survive this. She would put her life back together, learn from the experience and go forward. That's what she did.

She was a survivor.

* * *

After a long hard night dining and then sleeping without Annalise, Niko had endured a long, hard day without her, too. If he couldn't get through eighteen hours without her, how could he live the rest of his life without her?

He now understood what his brothers meant. Love for the right woman made a man feel whole. Without it, he had an aloneness that not even his family could fill. In Barcelona, he had accompanied his family to a cooking school presented by one of the area's famous restaurants, had chaperoned the youngest nieces and nephews through the children's museum and had people-watched with the twins, which was usually one of his favorite pastimes but today felt boring beyond measure.

Niko knew the problem wasn't with his activities but with his lack of a partner. If Annalise had been with him, it could have been one of his favorite days of all time. That's what being with Annalise did. It made every day his favorite day.

Niko kept glancing at the door to the party suite, even when he willed himself not to.

Marcus elbowed him. "Looking for someone, Uncle Niko? Someone special?"

He elbowed Marcus back. "Always."

Marcus cocked an eyebrow. "That's a different

Niko Christopoulos than the one I've known all my life."

"Just wait, nephew. Your time will come, sooner or later."

"In your case later."

Niko guessed he did seem old to a seventeen-year-old. "Better late than never."

That's what he'd tell Annalise when she finally arrived at Yiayia's party. And what he'd tell his family when he announced she was the one.

He glanced toward the door for the thousandth time in a minute. Where was she?

Niko hadn't caught a glimpse of her since last night at the late dinner seating when he'd sat with the family and she'd sat at the captain's table next to a computer nerd, smiling and nodding as if the twenty-five-year-old millionaire was the smartest man on the ship. Niko had to admit the kid probably was. Not that he had a right to be jealous, but...

If he only had that right...

Soon. Soon he would ask for that right.

Not that he would be the jealous type.

Had she really made a special effort to avoid looking at him, or had that been his ego aching, wanting her attention as she'd chatted the evening away with the computer nerd?

He would make sure Annalise never felt lonely

enough to even want to talk to another guy *in that special way* a woman talked to a man.

But he couldn't be there for her, couldn't watch sunsets with her, if he was in some field operation with no way to communicate except by short-wave radio carried to the highest local mountaintop. Could he ask her to wait for him?

That's why he'd never intended to fall in love. But life didn't always turn out the way a man planned it, did it?

She wasn't going to show. Despair followed on the heels of the devastating thought he kept trying to push away. What if it was one-sided? What if this was only a shipboard romance? And if it was more—it had to be more—where did they go with it from here?

What if she didn't show? What if she didn't care? She did, though, didn't she? Hadn't he seen it in her eyes? Felt it in her touch?

Niko caught himself staring at the door as he remembered how her eyes had flashed then squeezed tight in ecstasy the first time they'd come together.

It wasn't only sex. Not for him. Not for her either. All those times together, all those sunsets had to mean more than a vacation fling. He was as certain of that as he was that he was going to take another breath.

As he desperately tried to keep his attention on his excited six-year-old niece telling her rambling version of feeding a talking parrot, Niko felt a tingle in the back of his neck. Without turning, he knew she was there.

Suddenly, all the pieces fit into place inside him.

Yiayia confirmed it when she called out, "Dr. Annalise, welcome to my party. Let me get you some cake."

Her sundress with oversized orange and pink and purple flowers fit her better than his T-shirt but he missed seeing her wrapped in something that belonged to him.

Yiayia gave her one of the prized corner pieces of cake topped with an icing rose.

"For our special friend." Yiayia added a hug with the cake.

Over Yiayia's shoulder Annalise caught his glance. Shadows colored her eyes the same shade of sadness he was feeling.

"Thanks." Annalise's smile, even clouded, lit the darkest corners of his soul.

Before she could take a bite, Sophie demanded her attention. "Dr. Annalise, look at my picture. I'm feeding a parrot."

Niko watched her with Sophie, giving the child a lot more focused attention than he'd been able to. Annalise blended into his family as if she'd always been a part of them.

She was so good with children. He'd seen that at the refugee camp as well as with his own nieces and nephews.

She deserved a husband who could give her a house full of them.

Something very ugly inside him cringed at the thought of Annalise with another man. But it didn't have to be that way.

He could be that man who gave her babies.

He hadn't finalized the papers to sell his part of the practice. He could give her whatever she wanted.

Could he give up his dream, his calling to be a part of Doctors Without Borders, for her?

Or his other option—could he get up every morning, knowing he'd never see her again?

And the biggest question of them all. Did she love him like he loved her?

"To Yiayia!" His brother Stephen began the toasting. "May she have another great eight decades."

"To my grandson Stephen, who had the good sense to marry Phoebe!" Yiayia toasted back.

"To all the fine Christopoulos children, that they may be as wise and gracious and noble as their great-grandmother someday."

The older kids saluted Yiayia and the younger ones quickly followed suit with a little coaching.

"That's how it is in our family," Niko overheard Marcus explain to Annalise. "Like the Musketeers. All for one and one for all."

"To Dr. Annalise, who has graced us with her wisdom and compassion," Phoebe announced.

That was a toast Niko was pleased to drink to.

The toasting went on for almost an hour until every single family member had been covered, except for him.

He cringed, dreading the toast that was sure to come.

His brother Stephen was the one to deliver it.

"To Niko, the slow one of the family." Stephen held his glass high. "May he recognize love when it bites him on the butt then marry the woman and give her a household full of children before she figures out he's so much trouble."

Under the guise of saluting them all with his glass, he noticed Annalise fail to drink. What did it mean? Anything? Everything?

Annalise couldn't do it. She couldn't wish Niko into the arms of another woman. Thankfully, no one seemed to notice.

Phoebe splashed more wine into Annalise's glass

as Yiayia toasted her late husband, gone but not forgotten.

She made sure Annalise knew about his heroic exploits.

"My Leo, he was a brave and adventurous man. We travelled many places until we found the one that fit."

"Leo started the restaurant?"

"Oh, no, child. Leo couldn't cook any better than our Niko. He could never sit still either. Just like our Niko. Leo was a fireman. He died saving a pregnant woman. They called me to the hospital. He wasn't burned, at least not that we could tell, but the doctor said his lungs were too full of toxins. They didn't have all the fancy machines they have nowadays to save people. Two lives for one, he said, just before he died. Two lives for one." She looked sad but resigned and proud. "That woman's husband was a banker. He lent me the money to start the restaurant. My boys, Theo and Nicolos, they helped me after school. But then Nicolos became a policeman. We lost him in a bank robbery."

Yiayia glared at the Christopoulos men around her. "Until my grandsons, every generation has had a daredevil as far back as I can remember. But it stopped with my grandsons. I raised them to raise their own families, not to go and get themselves killed. It's a family tradition I'm proud to break."

Over Yiayia's head, Annalise shared a look with Niko, undertanding too well his reluctance to tell her about Doctors Without Borders. What would it do to Yiayia when she found out about his work?

Yiayia waved away the conversation. "Enough of the sad talk. This is a party. Niko, bring Annalise a plate of grapes and cheese and crackers. She will need some meat on her bones when she settles down to have her own children."

Niko loaded up a plate as directed, bringing it to her with a blank expression on his face. She could imagine the turmoil under the surface and her heart went out to him.

When Niko spoke of Doctors Without Borders, the resonance of his voice as well as the passion in his words told her how much it meant to him. When he described the work by saying it was the only time he felt like he was truly fulfilling his purpose for being alive, she easily believed him.

She also knew how much he loved his family. If she had such a wonderful family, it would wound her beyond healing to know she had to disappoint them to live the life that meant so much to her.

While Annalise regretted not having a family to

speak of, at least she had the freedom to make her own choices, guilt-free.

Annalise picked at the plate of food until Sophie called her to come look at how she could jump higher than her cousins.

Before the evening ended, Annalise was treated to at least one family story for each member of the Christopoulos clan, from the story about Stephen getting his tongue stuck on a block of dry ice to the one about how Niko hadn't told anyone about his motorcycle and how he'd been grounded for a week until he'd talked Yiayia into taking a ride on the back of it with him. Of course, she'd then forgiven everything and let him keep it.

Finally, Yiayia declared the party over when half the little ones were asleep on the chairs and the other half were running around in circles from being overtired.

All the brothers and sisters-in-law and their little ones hugged her goodnight, just like she was family. Annalise soaked it up. It would all be over too soon.

When they were the only ones left, Annalise asked Niko, "Want to go up top with me?"

"I'll follow you to the ends of the earth." While he'd meant it to be a teasing flirt, Niko had meant it from the bottom of his heart.

She grinned at him. "Tonight, the top deck will do for me."

"For me, too." Those moments alone with her each night gave him a calm serenity he'd never known before.

Tonight he needed that serenity to ease his angst. Niko had some deep thinking to do. If there was any other way...

But he'd heard it himself, verifying what he already knew. Every woman wanted babies, a home, a husband she could count on.

His grandmother had survived the tragedy of having to bury both a husband and a son. She'd raised her sons and then her grandsons alone. It had been a burden he could never ask any woman to carry.

With the work he did, the risk was always high that he wouldn't make it back home. He was willing to accept the odds for himself but he couldn't accept them for the woman he loved.

Giving up Doctors Without Borders would be like giving up his right arm. But giving up Annalise would be like giving up his heart.

CHAPTER SIXTEEN

MARCUS WAYLAID THEM before they got very far. "Uncle Niko, could I talk to you? In private?"

Marcus looked serious, old beyond his years. Dread made Niko's gut feel heavy. Whatever this was about, it wasn't going to be good.

Niko put on his professional stoicism. Teenagers could be spooked easily so he intended to play this as nonchalantly as possible. "Let's see if the library is deserted."

Annalise gave Marcus an encouraging smile. "You two go ahead. I'll catch up with you later, Niko."

"Dr. Annalise, I was hoping you'd weigh in on this, too. I could use a woman's opinion on how to deal with the females in the family."

Annalise looked confused but reluctantly agreed. "I'm not sure how much help I'll be but I'll give it a try."

Marcus sent a surreptitious glance toward his parents, got a thumbs-up from his twin, who had obviously been assigned to keep them busy, and grabbed a folder of papers from under a chair cushion.

He led the way to a secluded alcove half-obscured by a big potted palm. Niko and he straddled a lounge chair each and Niko had to grin at how much he and his nephew were alike.

But the grin didn't last long. Marcus pulled out a magazine and plopped it in Niko's lap.

On the front cover was a coastguard helicopter, hovering to pick up patients on a sinking home-made raft.

Niko remembered that day well. He identified the sleeve of his own jacket. He'd been just out of camera range for the shot. The photographer had caught the anxiety in the coastguard officer's eyes as he'd checked the straps on the carrier before the patient had been lifted up into the helicopter.

Niko was all too aware of Annalise studying the photograph. Did she understand the danger involved? By the seriousness in her eyes he thought she might.

"That's what I want to do, Uncle Niko."

"Be a doctor?"

"No. A coastguard pilot." He handed Niko a sheaf of papers. "The recruitment office sent me this paperwork. I can sign up now while I'm still in high school and get preferential consideration for the coastguard academy when I graduate. But there's a problem."

Without Marcus having to explain, Niko understood fully what the problem was. Stephen and Phoebe. They would be adamantly opposed to their son choosing such a dangerous career.

"Your parents won't like it at first but they love you, Marcus. There is nothing that will make them stop loving you."

"But Mom and Yiayia… What do you think, Dr. Annalise?"

"The women in your life are a lot stronger than you give them credit for."

Niko glanced down at the magazine cover's headline. "*U.S. Coastguard Teams with Doctors Without Borders to Make Daring Rescue*". "You want me to talk to them?"

"No. I don't need their permission. I'll be eighteen by the time I graduate. I won't need their signatures. But I need to get on the list now to take advantage of early enlistment." He handed Niko a blank form. "I want you to recommend me."

Niko blew out a breath. "Marcus, you know you've got my support in anything you want to pursue and I think you'll make a great coastguard pilot. But I won't go behind your parents' backs.

Hiding things from your family is the wrong thing to do."

He was all too aware of the sideways glance Annalise shot at him.

With the way Marcus stared at him, apparently she wasn't the only one who knew he had something to hide.

"You mean like paying for this trip and saying Yiayia won it?" Marcus flipped open the magazine to a photo of Niko precariously balanced on the disintegrating raft as he started an IV in the arm of a child. "Or like being part of Doctors Without Borders?"

Niko looked away from his nephew's eyes and swallowed. "The wrong thing for the right reasons."

Marcus nodded. "You gave us this trip because it's something Yiayia always dreamed of doing but we couldn't have afforded it. You figured everyone's pride would be too great and they wouldn't have accepted it as a gift."

Niko nodded. "That's about the size of it."

"And keeping this a secret?" Marcus pointed to the magazine. "Because you didn't want to worry anyone?"

The dread of family drama built in Niko's stomach. He felt as helpless as a child—as an eight-

year-old, to be exact. After all these years Niko
realized he associated family turmoil with that
time of tears and hysteria he'd barely survived.

Annalise put her hand on his shoulder, anchoring him and giving him strength.

Niko leaned into her touch as he looked into the
eyes of the nephew who looked up to him. "It's
time we came clean, both of us."

"You first?" Marcus challenged him.

"Me first." Niko threaded his fingers through
Annalise's. "Come with me?"

"This is a family matter. They won't appreci-
ate an outsider hearing about your financial ploy."
Annalise unthreaded her fingers from his, leaving
Niko feeling alone.

Usually she would be right, but his family had
taken her in as one of their own.

"You're not an outsider anymore."

"Then what am I?" She crossed her arms, hugging herself. "No. I don't do families."

The guarded look in her eyes stopped him from
saying more.

"Náste kalá." She reached up and kissed him on
the cheek. *"Antio."*

As the two of them walked towards the party room,
Marcus said, "You're going to tell them about pay-

ing for this trip and about Doctors Without Borders, right?"

"I'll tell them about the trip." Niko said aloud the decision he'd not wanted to face. "I'm resigning from the field."

"Why?"

"I want a—" Niko almost said *family*. But that was the easy answer, the answer he was programmed to give and Marcus was programmed to accept.

In the face of Marcus's honesty, Niko could do no less. "I can't ask a woman to take on my passion and travel with me or to stay at home and accept a part-time man in her life. So I'm giving up what I love most for who I love most."

"You're in love, Uncle Niko? With Dr. Annalise?"

Niko nodded.

Marcus cocked an eyebrow, looking so much like a typical Christopoulos male it made Niko smile. "The women in our lives *are* a lot stronger than we give them credit for. You should talk to her about it before you decide."

"Maybe I will, Marcus." Niko had to look away because he knew he wouldn't. Annalise would feel honor-bound to set him free. He would never put her in that position.

She would either tell him to go and she would wait for him at home—or she would just tell him to go. The first would wound her but he was certain the latter would kill him. While Marcus made arrangements with his brother to watch the little ones, Niko roused the adults and herded them into one of the family suites amid much confusion and speculation.

Once they were gathered, Niko tinged a half-full wine bottle with a fork to get everyone's attention.

"Marcus and I have some things to tell you." Niko took a deep breath, wishing he'd drunk the rest of the wine first. "I'll go first. Yiayia, the lady who delivered your sweepstakes check was an actress who owed me for medical work. I paid for this trip."

Thankfully, the suites on either side of his family's suite were no longer occupied as they all got uncivilly loud.

He told them everything—how much they meant to him for raising him and putting him through medical school, how he would be forever in their debt, how he deeply regretted disappointing them, but he had to be his own man. Everything had all tumbled out, as if the words couldn't escape him fast enough.

In the confusion and the turmoil Niko wasn't

quite sure how his confession came out so ungracefully. All he knew was that no matter how angry his family was with him, they still loved him, even if he insulted them by thinking he owed them anything. They did what they did for love—not for paybacks.

"Because that's what families do," Phoebe yelled at him when he tried to defend why he'd hidden his financial gift.

"Anything else you need to confess, Niko?" Yiayia asked. At his hesitation, his sisters-in-law added their own questions. Who could withstand the interrogation of the Christopoulos women *en masse*?

How he wished Annalise had been there to protect him when he said, "About those trips I've been taking…"

He made a full confession about Doctors Without Borders, even though he planned to resign for Annalise's sake.

Yes, Chistopoulos women were stronger than they looked.

They still weren't on board with Marcus's plan to make early application to the coastguard training academy. But when Stephen told Phoebe that at least Marcus was showing self-motivation and they wouldn't have to keep on him about keeping up his grades, Niko know they would eventually come round.

As always, his brothers forgave him everything, even expressing admiration, despite their wives' frowns.

Yiayia wasn't so kind about his involvement in Doctors Without Borders and his apparent bad influence on his nephew.

She wasn't speaking to him. In solidarity, neither were the other women. From past experience he knew their silent treatment wouldn't last beyond the night, and in the morning they'd be just as vocal as ever—which would not be a good thing if they were all still angry at him.

Yet he knew, when all was said and done, they were family—his family—and they loved him as much as he loved them. That's how the Christopoulos women were.

It was a comforting feeling.

But he had another woman on his mind who was giving him heartache.

Niko took the stairs two at a time, needing to see Annalise, to touch her, to hear her voice. Needing to reassure himself he was making the right decision.

As he made his nightly climb, he heard voices from above.

The top deck was filled with passengers watching Barcelona grow smaller and smaller as they pulled away from shore.

But it felt completely empty without Annalise.

What was that she'd said when she'd kissed him on the cheek? *"Náste kalá. Antio."*

Be well and goodbye.

She hadn't meant…she couldn't have meant…

There was still too much unsaid between them.

Packing had gone quickly. Everything Annalise wanted to take with her fit in a single suitcase. The rest she left for the crew, as was the custom.

She now stood on the dock at Barcelona's main port, watching the ship sail without her. The single suitcase made travelling easier as she caught a taxi to the airport.

Her last-minute decision meant she'd be flying to Athens for her interview with the local office of Doctors Without Borders tomorrow afternoon, instead of arriving by ship. Otherwise, everything was going as planned.

Except she hadn't expected her heart to be shattering into a million pieces.

How had she fallen in love so hard, so quickly?

Saying goodbye had been the hardest thing she'd ever done.

But it had been the right thing to do.

Annalise had left the medical suite in good hands.

Should an emergency occur, Annalise had total confidence in her P.A. and the ship would be in port each day with easy access to the best of medical care. And Sophie was surrounded by her loved ones, who would take very good care of her, just as they would if she were at home, while the Christopoulos family spent the week among the Greek isles. The thought made her smile. Those islands would never be the same again after they left.

After meeting them—after meeting Niko—she would never be the same again.

The further the ship sailed from shore, taking Niko away from her, the deeper she felt the pain from the shards of her broken heart. How could loving someone hurt so intensely?

A tour bus pulled up and Annalise realized she was standing under their sign.

"You want a ticket for the Night Lights of Barcelona tour, lady? Special admission into the museums and other tourist attractions."

"Sure. Why not?" Anything was better than wishing for what could never be.

Touring the galleries of Barcelona by herself, Annalise had never felt so lonely. Before Niko, she'd preferred to explore alone, taking her time to enjoy what she liked most.

But a thousand times during the evening she wanted to turn to Niko and say, "Look. What do you think?" and see his tiger eyes, hear his deep voice as they shared something of awe or beauty.

Could she ever share anything with anyone again?

Checking into the hotel, she saw a father with his two children, a daughter and a son, and it made her smile.

The son had a dimple that flashed like Niko's. She bet the boy got whatever he wanted when he turned on the charm.

Niko was perfect father material.

That's the future Niko's family wished for him. That's the future he should have. The future she could never give him. Reality tore her in two.

She loved Niko with every cell in her body. She loved him enough to let him go.

In her hotel room she wrapped herself in blankets and tried to warm her cold soul with memories. She closed her eyes, remembering the heat of his hands on her, the healing fire he'd built in her heart and in her body.

Niko had forever changed her for the better.

Logically she should be grateful for that and move on.

Her heart clenched in agony. As hard as she tried to be practical, her emotions kept seeping through.

One breath at a time. That's how she survived.

Annalise knew that about herself. She was a survivor.

And she could help others be survivors, too.

She had skills to give the world and for that she would continue to move forward in her life. She would do it in honor of the man who had shown her what love was.

She wished she would have told Niko about her plans. Wished she could have told him how much he meant to her. Wished there had been a better way than simply walking away. But she might have found the limit to her strength. Saying anything more than goodbye to Niko might have destroyed her.

Finally, as dawn broke through the darkness, she boarded the plane that would take her to her new future.

Niko was not in a good mood. Not being able to find the woman you loved did that to a guy. He'd stayed awake long after midnight, thinking, hoping, wishing she'd come knocking on his door. It hadn't happened.

As soon as morning had broken, he'd searched the ship—their favorite kiosk by the hot tubs, the video arcade and the skating rink, their place on the top deck, everywhere he could think to look.

It was a big ship but he'd always been able to find her when he looked for her before.

Where was she?

They hadn't made plans to meet, but he'd taken for granted—

He'd taken *her* for granted, assuming she would be there when he wanted her.

Fighting down panic, he found her P.A. in the medical suite.

"I don't know where she went, Dr. Christopoulos. She didn't tell me."

The P.A. said Dr. Walcott was done with her duties, had finished her contract. No, she couldn't give out Dr. Walcott's private cellphone number. No, she couldn't give out her cabin number either.

The P.A. gave him a sympathetic shrug. "If she's still on the ship, I'm sure she'll show up."

Niko turned away from the medical suite, stunned. Confused. Lost.

He wandered the ship, bow to stern, for hours.

Desolate, with no appetite, he joined his family for lunch. The smaller passenger list meant only one sitting. He would see her there. It would all be a bad coincidence that they hadn't connected. They would laugh about it. He would propose on the top deck. They would watch the sunset together. And his life would have meaning again.

But when he scanned the dining room, Annalise wasn't there.

The captain said he could give Niko no information. Then Helena took pity on Niko. She batted her eyelashes at the captain and asked sweetly on Niko's behalf. The captain agreed to have someone check the manifest to see if Annalise was still on the ship.

For now, all Niko could do was wait.

The meal with his family was as raucous as ever, reminding Niko what a misfit he was. While Niko barely mustered the will to swallow his soup, the rest of the family chattered around him.

As the wine began to flow, a steward came up to him, giving him a folded note.

Her contract with the ship is over. She vacated her quarters last night and disembarked in Barcelona. She's gone. I'm sorry, Helena

* * *

Niko waited impatiently for the ship to dock. His first stop in Athens would be the office of Doctors Without Borders. He would hand in his resignation and then search for Annalise.

He'd spend the rest of his life looking for her if he had to. And when he found her, he would do whatever he needed to do, be whoever he needed to be, to stay by her side.

Niko hurt deep down to the center of his soul. The ache was constant, like a thud on a hollow drum. He knew what it really was. It was the empty place where his heart used to be. Wherever Annaslise had gone, she had taken it with her.

Not that he hadn't given it to her freely. Only she had to be near him for it to go on beating, otherwise his life was just one day after the other with no heart in it.

Packets in hand, Annalise caught a taxi for her interview. If all went well, she would have a new job with Doctors Without Borders by the time she left Athens.

Once at their offices, Annalise signed the documents pledging herself for the coming year. The administrator gave her a genuinely grateful smile.

"You're perfect, Dr. Walcott. You've got emergency response training and emergency medical experience. You're used to making independent decisions and directing an ever-changing staff. You've even got all your shots."

Annalise gave her a rueful grin, remembering all the inoculations she'd had with the cruise line. "Sounds like I'm your woman, then."

"As soon as we finish all our background checks, we'll have your assignment for you. Not to worry, we'll put you with an experienced team leader until you're comfortable enough to be a team leader yourself."

Niko was a team leader. She had to grip her hands and bite her tongue to keep from requesting him. The wisest answer would be to specifically not ask for him.

It was a large, spread-out operation. What were the odds she would run into Niko on occasion? Would fate be cruel or kind?

In the end, she only nodded her understanding. "I'll be ready."

Emotion swamped Niko as he walked toward the Athens offices of Doctors Without Borders. Impatience overshadowed them all.

The sooner he got this excruciating decision behind him, the sooner he could begin his search for Annalise.

The doors opened and he blinked twice, sure his overwrought brain was playing tricks on him.

"Annalise?"

"Niko?" All blood drained from her face.

If he stood still, she would come to him, right?

After standing frozen, giving her space, giving her time that seemed to draw out for an eternity, he could stand still no longer.

He took three long, quick strides, bringing him next to her. He wanted to reach out and grab her, hold her and never let her go.

But she stood there looking so brittle, he thought if he touched her she might break into a thousand pieces.

"Hey." His throat was so dry from nerves, his voice almost cracked.

"Hey."

"I told them. Told them all about paying for the cruise, about my work, everything."

"And?"

"And it's okay. They're my family."

"You're a lucky man."

"Yes." He thought about how he had been ready to search to the ends of the earth for her and here she was. "Yes, I am."

She swallowed. "What are you doing here?"

"Remember all those toasts my family gave, the ones about me and babies?"

"How could I forget?" She wrapped her arms around herself and stared straight up into the cloudless blue sky. "Go on."

By the way Annalise barely breathed her words, Niko knew how crucial this was to her.

"I'm leaving Doctors Without Borders. Trying to have a family life, expecting my wife to raise the children while I'm gone for months at a time, it wouldn't be fair."

"Your family will be pleased."

Niko expected to see joy and maybe even appreciation for his sacrifice in Annalise's eyes. Instead, her jaw was set in determination as if she was about to swallow a dose of bad medicine.

"And you, Annalise? Aren't you pleased?" He waved his hands at the building behind them. "I'm doing this for you, for us. For our children."

"No. Not for us. There can be no *us*." Pain made the words cut like glass in her throat. "I've joined Doctors Without Borders. I'll be leaving as soon as I receive my assignment."

"Annalise, I can't let you do that. It's too dangerous."

"You can't let me? Niko, you have no choice in this."

"I can't lose you."

"You never had me," she lied. A piece of her soul would always belong to him. But it was better this way.

"What are you saying?" Niko stared at her as anger tumbled with sorrow and churned with disbelief. "With all that has been between us, I mean nothing to you?"

She pressed her lips together and shook her head. "No."

Her eyes, brimming with tears, and her voice, shaking and thick, said otherwise.

"Only honesty between us, remember?" He reached out for her. If her body said the same thing her lips said, he would know.

Gently, as if she would break at his touch, he cupped her chin. The energy was there. That connection he shared with no other person on earth pulsed under his fingertips. "You say I mean nothing to you. Then why the tears?"

"There was damage. I can't carry a child to term." She blew out a breath. "I've never said that out loud before."

"Annalise—"

She reached out to touch him, but dropped her hand before she made contact. "I've got to go."

"No." He was fierce in his answer, frowning at her, blocking her way.

"You would be such a good father but I'm not cut out to be a mother." She took two steps back and wrapped her arms around herself. "Please, Niko. I'm breaking into pieces here. Don't make this any harder."

"I don't want children." He frowned. "I thought you did."

She wiped at her eyes with the back of her hand. "Why did you think that?"

He seemed genuinely puzzled. "All women do, right?"

Through her tears, she gave him a watery smile. "Has anyone told you that you sometimes have a chauvinistic streak?"

"So you were just going to walk away from me? Without a discussion?"

"I couldn't ask you to choose, babies or me."

"You couldn't ask me? What about my right to choose?" He wiped at his own eyes. "But, then, you just said the same thing to me about Doctors Without Borders, didn't you? We're two of a pair, aren't we? Except for me, there is no choice. Without you, there is no me."

She stopped him with a finger over his lips. "Someday you'll want babies, Niko. You deserve babies. I can't give them to you."

He kissed her finger before clasping her hand, keeping her at his side. "If that day ever comes, there's more than one way to have children. We could adopt."

"You would do that for me?"

"Don't you understand, Annalise? I would do anything for you. Even resign from Doctors Without Borders. Anything."

She put her palm over his heart. "You were going to give up what you loved most for me?"

He covered her hand with his, feeling it warm under his touch as he held it tight against his chest. "I love you, Annalise. What I love most is whatever makes you happiest."

"What makes me happiest is being with you." She gave a nod back to the building. "Think they'll assign us together?"

"They will if they want to keep two very good doctors on staff." He looked down into her eyes. "Is this what you want? I'll give it up for you."

"I would never want you to cut out a part of yourself for me. I love you, Niko. The whole package."

"The whole package. No more holding back.

No more secrets—even if it is to protect the other person."

Annalise held out her free hand to him. When he wrapped his long, strong fingers around her delicate ones, she felt his strength surge through her. This was how it had always been between them. This was how it always would be.

"I'll make you a deal, Niko. I'll work on my communication skills if you'll work on yours."

He cocked an eyebrow at her. "It's going to take a lot of practice. A lot of togetherness."

She nodded. "A lot of patience and compromise."

"Sounds like a marriage to me."

"Are you asking?"

"No, I'm begging. Marry me, Annalise. Make my life whole."

"Yes, Niko. We'll be whole together."

* * * * *

Mills & Boon® Large Print
Medical

October

November

December

Mills & Boon® Large Print
Medical

January

DR DARK AND FAR-TOO DELICIOUS	Carol Marinelli
SECRETS OF A CAREER GIRL	Carol Marinelli
THE GIFT OF A CHILD	Sue MacKay
HOW TO RESIST A HEARTBREAKER	Louisa George
A DATE WITH THE ICE PRINCESS	Kate Hardy
THE REBEL WHO LOVED HER	Jennifer Taylor

February

MIRACLE ON KAIMOTU ISLAND	Marion Lennox
ALWAYS THE HERO	Alison Roberts
THE MAVERICK DOCTOR AND MISS PRIM	Scarlet Wilson
ABOUT THAT NIGHT...	Scarlet Wilson
DARING TO DATE DR CELEBRITY	Emily Forbes
RESISTING THE NEW DOC IN TOWN	Lucy Clark

March

THE WIFE HE NEVER FORGOT	Anne Fraser
THE LONE WOLF'S CRAVING	Tina Beckett
SHELTERED BY HER TOP-NOTCH BOSS	Joanna Neil
RE-AWAKENING HIS SHY NURSE	Annie Claydon
A CHILD TO HEAL THEIR HEARTS	Dianne Drake
SAFE IN HIS HANDS	Amy Ruttan

0913 LP 2P P2 M

MALPAS
2·10·13.

RINGLAND 12·11·14